Reel vs Real

Lise Gold
Ruby Scott

Happy Valentine's
For you, from my heart.
Ruby x.   #wholeheart

Happy Valentine's!
Hope you enjoy this
little labour of love
xxx Lise
spreadthelove

Copyright © 2025 by Lise Gold and Ruby Scott

All rights reserved.

No part of this book may be reproduced in any form or by any electronic or mechanical means, including information storage and retrieval systems, without written permission from the author, except for the use of brief quotations in a book review.

Chapter One

The thing about watching other people's perfect lives is that it makes your own feel impossibly small. While Nicole and Jen posted their sunrise yoga to eight hundred thousand followers, Ana changed Mrs. Rodriguez's catheter. Lately, she'd become obsessed with their Instagram feed, their beautifully curated 'morning routines' a constant assault on her senses. Each post felt like a tiny, venomous dart aimed at her soul.

"You're thinking about those internet girls again, aren't you?" Mrs. Rodriguez said, her voice thin and sharp. The old woman, a resident here longer than Ana had been alive, knew her well.

"Just working, Mrs. R.," Ana said, securing the catheter, her mind already drifting back to her phone. Five years of wiping, cleaning, and changing had turned even the most personal care into just another task to check off. She doubted Nicole and Jen, with their manicured hands and designer clothes, had ever encountered such things.

Her phone buzzed again, and she surrendered. Another post: Nicole and Jen, lounging in silk pajamas with green smoothies, looking loved-up in the morning light. "Rise and shine with my love #morningroutine #couplegoals #blessed 🤍," the caption chirped.

Ana checked her watch: 6:30 AM. Day shift would be coming in soon. While Nicole and Jen were starting their serene morning routine, all Ana could think about was crawling into bed. At least she'd get to say good morning to Dani before she left for her shift at Garcia's.

*　*　*

The kitchen, a cramped corner defined by a scarred countertop in their studio, was a cluttered mess of bills and takeout containers. But the sight of Dani, still half-asleep, warm and inviting in their bed, was a balm that no Instagram post could ever replicate.

"What time is it?" Dani mumbled, her voice thick with sleep, a husky undertone that still made Ana weak in the knees.

"Early enough that the roaches are having a fiesta," Ana said. She tossed her scrubs into the overflowing laundry basket. The building's washing machines were, as usual, out of order. "Had to cover Jenny's shift again. Third time this month."

Another buzz, impossible to resist. This time, it was a picture of Nicole and Jen, locked in a morning kiss, their bedroom bathed in sunlight, fresh flowers artfully arranged, matching mugs in hand. "Every morning I fall in love all over again. #morningritual #authenticlove 🤍."

Dani pushed herself up, the quilt pooling around her waist, revealing a faded Selena Gomez T-shirt. "Put that away and come here," she said, patting the space beside her.

"We only have twenty minutes before I have to head to work."

"Mmm... I need a quick shower. I smell like disinfectant and the twilight years." But Ana was already moving toward the bed, drawn to the warmth radiating from Dani.

"You smell like hard work and dedication," Dani said, pulling her down for a kiss. Her lips were soft, warm from sleep, and Ana melted into her touch.

A loud bang from the upstairs neighbor shattered the moment—a daily reminder of the building's less-than-soundproof construction. Dani broke the kiss, chuckling. "Mrs. Hernandez's morning Zumba?"

"Or she's finally done in Mr. Hernandez," Ana said, reluctantly pulling away. "I'll make us coffee."

"Thanks, baby." Dani grinned as she stretched. "The perks of having a girlfriend working night shifts."

Ana rolled her eyes, but she couldn't stop the smile tugging at her lips. "Just a couple of early birds, you and me."

"Nah, girl. Early birds get the worm. We get the commute. But I'll take it as long as I get to see your beautiful face every morning."

Ana felt the familiar, sweet ache in her chest. Exhaustion tugged at her, but the knowledge that they'd finally achieved their own little place made it all worthwhile. She couldn't imagine wanting anything else.

She filled the kettle, the water sputtering as it heated on the ancient hotplate. The muffled sounds of the neighbor's TV, the drone of the morning news, bled through the thin walls.

While she waited, she picked up her phone again, thumbing past shift reminders and overdue bills to open

Instagram. The app sprang to life, filled with perfect smiles, artfully arranged meals, and sun-drenched selfies.

One post snagged her attention. Nicole and Jen, limbs entwined on a crisp white duvet, their hair a picture of effortless disarray, their skin glowing. "Lazy mornings with my love #blessed #couplegoals 🩶," the caption read.

A knot tightened in Ana's stomach, a complex blend of yearning and something sharper, almost like resentment. What would it be like, she wondered, to wake up to that? No alarms, no obligations, no worries about the next paycheck.

"Whatcha looking at?" Dani asked, padding up behind her, slipping her arms around Ana's waist and hooking her chin over her shoulder. The familiar weight of her, solid and warm, anchored Ana back to reality.

"That couple I follow. Nicole and Jen."

Dani hummed, her breath tickling Ana's ear. "The bougie ones with the supposedly perfect life?"

"Yeah. I just... I look at them sometimes, and I think, damn. That must be nice, you know? To have what they got."

Dani was quiet for a moment, her arms tightening around Ana's middle. "You want that kinda life, *mija*? For real?"

Ana sighed, locking her phone and setting it aside. The kettle was starting to whistle, the sound shrill. She turned in the circle of Dani's arms, reaching up to loop her own around her neck.

"Nah," she said softly, touching her forehead to Dani's. "I mean, maybe sometimes I wonder. But at the end of the day? I got everything I need right here."

"Damn straight." Dani's smile was brighter than any Instagram filter as she leaned in to capture Ana's lips in a slow, sweet kiss. "You and me against the world, baby," she murmured as they parted. "That's all we need."

Ana poured the instant coffee, stirring in powdered creamer and enough sugar to make her teeth ache. Dani was right. This life of theirs, with its peeling wallpaper and leaky faucets and endless double shifts, it wasn't flashy.

But it was real. It was theirs.

And in the end, that was what mattered most.

Chapter Two

Sunrise, a soft gold, illuminated Nicole through the floor-to-ceiling windows of their Calabasas home. She inhaled deeply, palms smoothing the silk of her robe—a sponsored piece she was contractually obligated to showcase in at least three more posts this month. This performance of peace was her daily ritual, though lately, it felt contrived.

Her reflection stared back at her, every detail crafted: the artfully tousled honey-blonde hair, the "woke up like this" makeup that had taken forty minutes to achieve, the robe strategically arranged. Behind her, their bedroom was meticulously styled—white linens, carefully placed throw pillows, a self-help bestseller on the nightstand.

Everything in its place. Everything perfect. Or at least, perfect for the camera.

Behind her, she heard Jen in the kitchen. The coffee maker hissed and sputtered—the basic one they actually used, not the expensive model they showcased in their posts. The clink of dishes seemed unusually loud, carrying a tension Nicole didn't want to acknowledge. She sensed a slowness in Jen's movements, a weariness that had been creeping into their home in recent weeks.

Nicole pushed the thought away, as she pushed away all thoughts that didn't serve the brand. She picked up her phone. The screen glowed with notifications—comments, likes, partnership offers. Their latest post had performed adequately, but "adequately" wasn't enough anymore. They needed more. Always more.

Her gaze drifted to the bed, where a beautiful breakfast awaited its photo op. Sliced fruit was arranged artfully, a single, perfect rose from Jen's garden sat in the center, and a steaming pot of coffee they probably wouldn't drink completed the scene. The real breakfast—slightly burnt toast—sat cooling in the kitchen.

"Jen?" she called out. "Can you come here a sec?"

Silence stretched between them, then the soft padding of footsteps. Jen appeared in the doorway, and Nicole's heart clenched. She was already dressed for work in sturdy boots caked with yesterday's mud, a faded green T-shirt, and jeans with grass stains on the knees. She looked beautiful—real, solid, alive—and completely wrong for their brand.

"What's up?" Jen asked, her gaze flicking to the staged breakfast, then back to Nicole. There was a question in her eyes, a hint of something that looked dangerously like resignation.

Nicole forced a bright smile, willing it to reach her eyes. "I thought we could do a little morning shoot. You know, couple's breakfast in bed and all that jazz."

She watched the resistance flicker across Jen's face, the subtle tightening of her jaw. It was a familiar tension between them, but lately, it felt more forced, more strained.

"Now?" Jen said. "I was going to head to work. I've got

the Peterson's garden, and then the new client in Beverly Hills—"

"It'll only take a few minutes," Nicole said. She glanced at her phone, checking the light. "Come on, it's perfect right now. Golden hour. We need this content, babe."

What she didn't say was that they needed more than content. They needed the sponsorship money, desperately. The mortgage on this house they couldn't really afford. The car payments. The ever-climbing credit card bills. It was all held together by a delicate web of partnerships and posts. One missed opportunity, one dropped contract, and it could all come crashing down.

Jen must have seen something in her eyes because she sighed, a soft, weary sound that was becoming all too familiar. She approached the bed, careful not to disturb the arrangement, kicked off her boots, and got under the covers. "Great. Now I'm staining the covers with my dirty clothes."

"Don't worry about that. Just pull them up so only your face is visible." Nicole raised her phone. "Pretend you're enjoying a lazy morning with your girlfriend."

Jen complied, but the strain was evident. Nicole snapped a few photos, her lips pursing. "Can you try to look a little more... natural?"

"This is me being natural," Jen said, rolling her eyes.

The comment stung, piercing Nicole's composure. "That's not what I meant. I just want us to look happy, you know? Like we're in love."

"Right. Because that's what really matters, isn't it? How it looks."

Nicole flinched. "You used to love taking pictures with me," she said defensively. "You never had a problem with it until recently."

"You're right. When it was just you and me. What I

loved was making memories with you, Nicole, not staged scenes. But since you quit your job to do this full-time, it's become like a chore. It means nothing anymore."

Nicole swallowed, her throat suddenly tight. "Jen..." she began. "This is important, Jen. It's for our future. We make twice as much money doing this."

Jen's gaze hardened. "Our future? What about our present? What about right now? What about just having a coffee together before I head to work? Use our time to talk to each other instead of all this staging."

Nicole felt a cold dread creeping into her stomach. This wasn't supposed to happen. They were supposed to be a team, a power couple, a success story. Not this... this unraveling.

"I'm just trying to make things better," she mumbled. "For both of us."

"For your followers, you mean?" Jen said. "For the brands? For the algorithm?"

Nicole felt tears prick her eyes and blinked them back furiously. "This is what we do, Jen. This is how we make a living. We're influencers. It's who we are."

"Is it?" Jen asked, her voice laced with a quiet fury. "We spend our days chasing likes. We've become caricatures of ourselves, ghosts in our own lives. Is that who you want to be?"

She looked at the breakfast, the props, the image Nicole was so desperately trying to project. "This is ridiculous." She rose, setting down the prop coffee with a sharp clatter, and put her boots back on. "I have to go. I'm already late."

Nicole watched her leave, footsteps retreating down the hallway, each one echoing like a small defeat. She looked at the photos on her phone. There it was, in every shot: the cracks in their curated facade, the growing distance in Jen's eyes, the strain in her smile. They were becoming harder to conceal, impossible to filter away.

Through the windows, the sun continued its climb, and the hum of a distant lawnmower filled the air. Millions of lives unfolded beyond their windows, each with its own story. She imagined countless seemingly perfect couples, each telling their own flawless love stories.

A sense of loneliness washed over Nicole. She felt adrift, disconnected from Jen, from the world around her, trapped in a gilded cage of her own making.

She just wished she knew how to make their relationship real again.

Chapter Three

Money. It always came down to money.

Nicole stared at their bank balance on her phone, the numbers blurring as tears welled up. Surrounded by the sterile perfection of their Calabasas kitchen—all marble and gifted appliances that felt more like shackles—the reality was inescapable. Three maxed-out credit cards. An overdue mortgage. Plummeting follower engagement.

The initial surge had been exhilarating—a meteoric rise in followers, lucrative brand deals pouring in. It had felt like a golden age, a time of limitless possibilities. Nicole had quit her job, convinced that their influencer empire would effortlessly sustain them. Now, the illusion of effortless success felt like a cruel joke.

An email pinged, offering a brief flicker of hope. A sponsorship. Her heart leaped, then sank. King Ranch, Texas. A "luxury ranch experience" weekend. The proposed compensation was... meager. She checked the figure again, certain she'd misread it.

"No," she whispered, scrolling through the details. "Is that all?"

"What's wrong?" Jen said, startling her. She stood framed in the doorway in her work clothes, a well-worn thermal mug in hand.

"A place called King Ranch in Texas wants us for a weekend," Nicole said. "A sponsored stay. It looks good. Great food, horse-riding, a beautiful ranch..."

"Texas?" Jen said, her eyebrows rising. "In January?"

"It's a group thing. Several influencer couples." She forced a smile. "Could be good exposure. They pay, and flights are included."

Jen's expression darkened. "When?"

"Next weekend."

"No." Jen turned toward the door. "I've got that wedding garden to finish, and then the Petersons' new landscaping—"

"Babe, please." Nicole's voice cracked. "We need this."

"What we need is for me to work. My actual job. The one that pays steady money."

"Pennies," Nicole snapped. "You make pennies compared to what we could be making—"

"Don't." Jen's voice was low, dangerous. "Don't you dare dismiss my work. I've poured years into building my own business, and if you hadn't insisted on living such a lavish lifestyle in Calabasas, I could easily support us."

Nicole winced and looked away. She knew Jen was right. Through the window, the rhythmic whirring of a hedge trimmer cut through the silence. Their neighbor's gardener was sculpting hedges into cubes, and the irony of that was palpable.

"How bad is it?" Jen asked.

Nicole swallowed. "It's bad."

"The credit cards?"

"Maxed."

"The mortgage?"

Nicole's silence was answer enough.

Jen carefully set down her mug and perched on a stool next to her. "Show me."

Nicole handed over her phone, watching Jen scroll through their accounts. "Jesus, Nic. Why didn't you tell me?"

"I thought I could handle it. The sponsored posts were doing well, and then—"

"And then they weren't."

Nicole nodded, her throat tight. "Our engagement is down. Brands are looking for new faces. Younger couples. Traveling couples."

"Like those who pretend to live out of a luxurious campervan?" Jen's laugh was brittle. "At least that would be affordable."

"Jen—"

"How much?" Jen cut her off. "The ranch. How much are they offering?"

"Eighteen hundred dollars," Nicole said, watching her face fall. "Two days, one night. In return, they want ten posts mentioning the ranch and the rights to use our pictures on their website."

"That's not much for an off-site, especially if you hand over commercial imagery." Jen shrugged, a hint of bitterness in her voice. "But I guess it's more than the pennies I make in two days."

"It's not just about the money," Nicole said, ignoring Jen's dig. "It's exposure. Connections. There'll be other influencers there, bigger names. If we network, maybe get noticed—"

"Right," Jen said. "Because that's worked so well before." She picked up her coffee again and headed for the door. She stopped. Without turning around, she said, "Fine. Book it. Not like we have a choice, right?"

"Babe—"

"Just... book it." The door closed behind her with a soft click that somehow hurt more than a slam would have. They were drifting apart—she felt it with every stilted conversation, every averted glance, every night they fell asleep without a kiss. When was the last time Jen had touched her, really touched her? Not just a quick peck goodbye, but the way she used to—like she couldn't get enough. The resentment was palpable in Jen's every tight-lipped response, a direct result of their spiraling financial crisis. But Nicole would make it right. She had to.

She slid off the designer bar stool—another gifted item, another obligation. Her phone buzzed: a DM from Melissa St. Clair, one of the biggest lifestyle influencers on Instagram.

"Heard about King Ranch! So excited to finally meet you two lovebirds in person. Your authentic sapphic content is exactly what we need right now. Speaking of which... got something special planned around Valentine's Day. A little cruise on my yacht. Very exclusive. Think about it?"

Nicole stared at the message, her heart racing. A yacht cruise. With Melissa St. Clair. The exposure would be incredible. She knew exactly why Melissa had reached out. Her 800k followers were barely half of Melissa's own, but they filled a convenient niche in her curated social circle. They were the "diverse" couple, a tasteful splash of queer representation in Melissa's collection of influencer friends. If playing that role meant access to Melissa's audience and a chance to regain their former glory, she'd smile for every photo.

Through the window, she watched Jen climb into her beat-up truck, the one she refused to replace because "it still runs fine." As she pulled away, Nicole could almost hear her voice: "Token lesbians. That's all we are to them."

She looked down at her phone again. The ranch offer. The yacht invitation. The overdue mortgage notice.

With shaking fingers, she typed her response to the ranch: "We would be delighted to join. Please send me the deets."

Then to Melissa: "That sounds amazing! I'll discuss it with Jen and get back to you ASAP. #blessed"

Then she opened their joint calendar and deleted Jen's gardening appointments for next weekend, her stomach churning as she erased the numbers, replacing Jen's promised income with a single entry: "King Ranch Sponsorship."

Jen was right. They didn't have a choice.

Chapter Four

"Are you sure about this?" Ana asked, her voice muffled as she struggled into the borrowed white button-down. It was slightly too big, a hand-me-down from Dani's cousin who'd quit his waiter job at the country club last summer.

"Yeah. Mike's cool. You said you were sick of nightshifts, so I thought you could try this out. See if you like it." Dani leaned against the doorframe, already dressed in her chef's whites, her dark hair pulled back in a tight bun. "Garcia's got the contract last minute. Their regular people canceled. Rich folks still gotta eat, even at their fancy ranch."

"But I'm not qualified-" Ana tugged at the shirt, trying to make it look professional. "I don't have any experience."

"You can hold a tray, right?" Dani crossed the small bathroom, her hands replacing Ana's on the buttons. "But there's another reason I thought you might want to come." Her lips quirked into a mischievous smile. "Heard through Mike the guests are influencers. Including a certain couple you can't seem to stop following..."

Ana gasped. "Wait. Nicole and Jen? They're going to be there?"

"Got it in one." Dani chuckled. "Thought you might want to see how your Instagram obsession looks in real life."

"Oh my god." Ana's stomach did a complicated flip. "No. No way. I can't—I mean, what if I drop something? What if I make a fool of myself? What if—"

"What if you realize they're just regular people who happen to have a really good camera?" Dani finished buttoning the shirt and stepped back. "Besides, you'll be too busy working to go full fangirl on them."

Ana caught her reflection in the mirror. The borrowed shirt, her hair pulled back, the dark circles under her eyes barely concealed. Her heart fluttered. She was going to meet them. Nicole and Jen. The couple she'd followed for over a year, whose perfect life she'd admired from afar.

Later, they made the drive to King Ranch. It took almost two hours. They left before dawn while the stars were still bright in the Texas sky. Ana spent the entire trip memorizing the briefing Dani had given her: six influencer couples, a luxury ranch experience, photos and content creation throughout the day, with breakfast, lunch, and dinner service.

"Just remember," Dani said as they pulled into the staff parking area, gravel crunching under the tires of their old Civic, "don't stare. Don't ask for photos. Don't get personal."

The morning air was crisp, carrying the scent of sage and mesquite. Ana followed Dani through the back entrance, trying to calm her racing heart. The kitchen was already bustling, and through the service window, she could see the dining room being set up—crystal glasses, fresh flowers arranged with meticulous care.

"Dani!" A voice called out. "I need you on appetizer prep. And who's this?"

"My girlfriend," Dani said. "Thought we could use the extra hands. We're always short-staffed when it comes to last-minute gigs."

The manager, Mike, looked Ana over with tired eyes. "You done service before?"

"Yes, sir," Ana lied, straightening her stance and channeling her nursing home professionalism. "Two years."

He nodded wearily. "Fine. Help with breakfast setup. But if anyone asks—"

"I work for Garcia's," Ana finished. "Got it."

The next hour passed in a blur of activity. Ana fell into the rhythm easily enough—it wasn't so different from her nursing home rounds, really. Just with better china and fewer bedpans. Then she heard it. That laugh—the one she'd heard in countless Instagram stories. It was Nicole. She was even more stunning in person, dressed in stylish western wear. It was a feminine take on cowboy chic, probably costing more than Ana made in a month. Jen was with her, looking less comfortable in similar attire. Her usual practical clothes were replaced with something that screamed "authentic ranch experience."

"Babe," Dani whispered as she passed by with a tray of miniature quiches, "stop staring."

But it was hard not to. Especially when Ana could see what the cameras never showed. They didn't radiate that ethereal glow from their filtered photos. Instead, they looked startlingly human, with slight shadows under their eyes and the occasional nervous glance at each other. Still beautiful, Ana thought, but beautiful in the way real people were.

"Coffee service," Mike announced, pushing a carafe into Ana's hands. "Table three."

Ana's pulse raced. Table three. Nicole and Jen's table. "Just breathe," she told herself, approaching. "It's just coffee."

"I can't believe they expect us to actually ride horses," Nicole said as Ana approached. "I can't ride. I'll look terrible. Do you know what that could do to my engagement?"

"Heaven forbid your engagement suffers," Jen muttered, then louder, "Coffee, please."

Ana's hands shook slightly as she poured. This close, she could see the exhaustion on Nicole's face, the small scar on her forehead.

"Are those fresh flowers?" Nicole asked, fingering the centerpiece.

"Yes, ma'am," Ana said. "Brought in this morning."

"Nice." Nicole pulled out her phone. "Jen, lean in. The light's amazing right now."

Ana watched as Jen's face transformed, a smile appearing on demand. "Let's not forget to tag the ranch," Nicole said, her own camera-ready smile in place. "I'll focus on the authentic Texas experience."

"Right," Jen said, her voice flat. "Authentic." As Ana stepped back, she caught Jen's eye for just a moment—a flicker of exhaustion, a hint of sadness, quickly masked by that practiced smile.

She found Dani in the kitchen, prepping garnishes.

"Well?" Dani asked, not looking up from her work. "Everything you hoped for?" Ana frowned, thinking about Jen's tired eyes, the performance of it all.

"No," she said softly. "Not really."

Dani's hands stilled. She looked up, meeting Ana's gaze. "Good," she said simply, and went back to her garnishes.

Through the service window, Ana watched Nicole positioning her coffee cup just so, angling for the right shot. Jen sat beside her, scrolling through her phone, looking like she wished she were anywhere else.

"Hey," Dani said, pulling her attention back. "Will you chop these lemons into wedges for me? Unless you'd rather watch the show."

Ana smiled, moving to join her girlfriend. Their fingers brushed as Dani handed her a knife, and that small touch held more warmth than all the filtered photos in the world. "No," she said. "I'm good right here."

Chapter Five

The rest of the breakfast service unfolded in a flurry of coffee refills and increasingly specific requests. "More edible flowers on this one," and "Could we get some pomegranate seeds for color?" and "Do you have any purple basil?"

Half the food ended up as props rather than sustenance—meticulously styled plates photographed from every angle, barely tasted before being sent back for the next arrangement. What a waste, Ana thought, watching another barely-touched plate return to the kitchen. But then again, all the more for them. Garcia's always let Dani take home leftovers, and smoked salmon was a luxury they couldn't afford.

She found herself drawn to Nicole and Jen's table, stealing glances and absorbing every detail. The way Nicole paused between bites to capture the right angle of her avocado toast. How she'd touch Jen's arm when other influencers approached, seamlessly shifting their poses into couple mode.

But it was the moments between the poses that held her

attention. Jen's smile would falter when Nicole looked away. Nicole's shoulders held a subtle tension when Jen's responses came a beat too slow.

"Order up!" Dani's voice broke through her observations. "Table three."

Ana's pulse quickened at the thought of approaching their table again.

"You're staring again," Dani whispered as she handed over the plates. "They're gonna notice."

"I'm not—" Ana started to protest, but Dani was already turning back to her prep station.

Ana approached the table, balancing the fresh plates. Nicole was mid-story, her hands moving animatedly as she spoke to another influencer couple—the Mitchells, Ana recognized them.

"And then," Nicole said, her voice dropping to a conspiratorial whisper, "Melissa messages me about this Valentine's cruise. Super exclusive."

"On her yacht?" Mrs. Mitchell's eyebrows rose. "The *Pacific Dream?*"

"Mmhmm." Nicole's smile was dazzling. "She says they're desperate for our authentic sapphic content."

Jen's fork clattered against her plate. "Excuse me," she said, standing abruptly. "It's warm in here. I need some air."

Ana barely managed to step back in time as Jen pushed past her.

"She's just nervous about the horse riding later," Nicole said smoothly, though a flash of hurt crossed her eyes. "Jen's more of a garden girl than a ranch girl."

The Mitchells offered polite laughs, but an awkward undercurrent lingered. Ana busied herself setting down and arranging their plates, hyperaware of every movement.

"Speaking of the yacht," Mrs. Mitchell said, clearly

trying to move past the uncomfortableness, "have you decided what you're wearing? Melissa usually goes for that luxury nautical vibe."

"Oh, God." Nicole's laugh tinkled like crystal. "Don't even get me started on the packing situation. My stylist is having a meltdown…"

Ana lingered, pretending to adjust table settings nearby, listening intently. A luxury yacht. Stylists. Custom wardrobes. It sounded like a dream.

Back in the kitchen, Dani was chopping tomatoes. "Having fun?" she asked, not looking up.

"They've been invited onto a yacht for Valentine's Day," Ana said, unable to keep the excitement from her voice. "Can you imagine?"

Dani's knife stilled. "No," she said quietly. "I can't."

Something in her tone made Ana pause. "Dani…"

"Break time," Mike announced, cutting through the moment. "Fifteen minutes. Be back at eleven."

They found a quiet spot behind the kitchen, sharing a package of Takis and a Coke.

"I'm sorry," Ana said finally. "I know I'm being…intense about them."

Dani sighed, her shoulders softening. "I just…" she hesitated. "I see how you look at their life. Like it's some kind of fairy tale." She flinched, meeting Ana's eyes. "Sometimes I wonder if what we have isn't enough for you. If I'm not enough."

Ana's stomach dropped. She reached for Dani's hand, shaking her head vigorously. "No, no. That's not what I meant at all. I love our life. I love you more than anything in this world. You know that, right?" She squeezed Dani's hand. "I was just talking about… you know, the stuff. The luxuries, the freebies. Not what really matters."

Dani turned the Takis bag in her hands, her usual confidence faltering. "Sometimes when you're scrolling through their feed, though... I see this look on your face—"

"That's just me being dazzled by shiny things, like a magpie." Ana touched Dani's cheek. "But you? You're my person. I love that we split that one good pillow we have. And that you pretend not to notice when I steal your hoodies."

"I notice. I just like how they look on you." Dani finally smiled. "But shiny things don't equal happiness."

Ana frowned. "What do you mean?"

"Come on, baby. You saw it, too. The tension between them?" Dani popped another Taki in her mouth. "And about the yacht? Jen looks like she'd rather jump off it than spend a day with those people."

"Yeah, she seems a little uncomfortable... Maybe she's just shy," Ana said, though a nagging feeling tugged at her. She remembered how Jen had pushed past her. The strain in Nicole's eyes.

"Maybe." Dani didn't sound convinced. "Or maybe it's all just for show."

Before Ana could respond, the back door opened. "Break's over!" Mike called. "Lunch service in thirty!"

Ana stood, brushing the bright orange Taki dust from her hands. But as she turned to follow Dani, a sound caught her attention. From around the corner of the building, just out of sight, came the sound of someone crying. She hesitated, then cautiously peered around the edge.

It was Jen, phone pressed to her ear. "I can't do this anymore, Mom. The debt, the constant performing... I don't even recognize us anymore. But Nicole won't listen. She thinks she can solve everything with that stupid account of hers..." Her voice cracked, giving way to sobs.

Ana pulled back quickly, her heart pounding. She hadn't meant to hear that—hadn't meant to glimpse behind that particular curtain.

"You coming?" Dani called from the doorway.

"Yeah," Ana said, shaking off the moment. Jen's quiet sobs echoed in her mind, a stark contrast to the bright and shiny facade she'd admired for so long.

Through the pass, she could see Nicole holding court at her table, her laugh carrying across the dining room. Her poses were effortless, her smile dazzling. Ana couldn't help but wonder—what was real, and what was just for show?

Chapter Six

The winter sun beat down on King Ranch's show ring, turning the stirred-up Texas dust into a golden haze. Nicole shifted on the wooden fence, trying to find a comfortable yet photogenic angle—not easy in the tight jeans and suede vest.

Her phone screen showed her latest post from breakfast: twenty-three thousand likes and climbing. Good, but not great. Not enough. Comments rolled in—"Couple goals!" and "Living the dream!"—but each one felt more hollow than the last.

In the ring, Jen was mounting a horse for their scheduled riding lesson. Despite her protests, she looked natural up there, her body relaxed, moving with the animal. The photographer circled them, capturing every moment.

"Love the authenticity!" Melissa St. Clair called from her perch on the fence nearby. "So raw, so real."

Nicole's smile felt plastered on. Raw and real. Like anything about this day was real. She watched as Jen guided her horse around the ring, following the instructor's directions. Even in the designer western wear Jen hated—and had initially refused to wear—she moved with a grace that made Nicole's chest ache. This was the woman she'd fallen in love with—strong, capable, unaffected. When had that stopped being enough?

"So, about the yacht," Melissa said, sliding closer. "You guys are coming, right?"

"We'd love to of course. Jen just needs to check her work schedule," Nicole lied.

"It will be worth it. The content opportunities alone..." Melissa's long manicured nails tapped against the fence. "And between us? The sponsoring brands? Let's just say it could be very lucrative for your bank balance."

The mention of money made Nicole's throat tighten. Their bank balance flashed in her mind: red numbers, growing larger each day.

"Speaking of which," Melissa continued, her voice dropping to a conspiratorial whisper, "that gardening business of Jen's? So charming, but hardly sustainable for someone of your caliber. Have you considered—"

"I need to make a call," Nicole cut her off, pushing herself off the fence. She couldn't listen to this. Not now. She headed toward the main house, her boots kicking up dust. Behind her, she heard the instructor praising Jen's natural seat, punctuated by the rapid click of the photographer's camera.

The service entrance was propped open, cool air and kitchen sounds spilling out. Nicole slipped inside, seeking a moment's refuge. The prep area was bustling with activity. That waitress from breakfast—the one who'd looked at her with such admiration—was helping a dark-haired chef arrange plates.

"No, like this," the chef said, guiding the waitress's

hands as she arranged the garnish. The intimacy of the gesture made Nicole look away.

"Nicole?"

She turned. Jen stood in the doorway, hat in hand, face flushed from riding. "What are you doing back here?"

"I—" Nicole hesitated. What could she say? That she was hiding? That watching Jen ride had reminded her of who they used to be before filters and followers had taken over their lives? She longed for that connection again, that feeling of being completely in sync. Back when they were a real team, not just performing teamwork for likes. When they shared the same goals.

Instead, she said, "Melissa wants an answer. About the yacht."

Jen's face closed off. "Of course she does."

"It's a huge opportunity, babe. The connections alone—"

"Right." Jen's voice was flat. "Connections."

Behind them, the kitchen staff were pretending not to listen, but Nicole was acutely aware of their presence. The waitress froze, a garnish hovering over a plate. "Not here," she said quietly. "Please."

Jen laughed, a short, bitter sound. "Why not? Isn't this authentic enough for you?" The words hit like a slap, and Nicole took a step back.

"Jen, please. Just say yes. One last time."

"Can't you go alone? I have a business to run." Jen's eyes narrowed as she regarded Nicole. "You know what? Everything was fine when we both had our own things going. When you were in creative marketing, and I was building my business from the ground up. Remember that tiny kitchen in West Hollywood? How we'd make dinner and gossip about our clients?" Her voice cracked slightly. "We used to laugh so much, Nic. Remember that wobbly IKEA table? We'd sit there and just... talk. No phones, no poses, no styled breakfast plates. Just us, sharing our day." She shook her head. "What the fuck happened to us?"

"Come on, Jen." Nicole's voice took on a desperate edge. "You can't tell me you don't prefer what we have now. The house in Calabasas? Remember how excited we were when we first saw that kitchen? And now we have two cars. We can go anywhere, stay at the nicest hotels..." She trailed off, searching Jen's face for any sign of agreement. "We used to dream about stuff like this, didn't we?"

"I liked hitching a ride to work with you," Jen said. "I liked how you'd blast your terrible pop music and we'd get coffee at that corner shop that never got your name right." She crossed her arms. "And this isn't a vacation, Nic. Remember Hawaii? That wasn't a vacation either. I spent half the week posing like a trained monkey. We hardly got a moment to ourselves."

"That's not fair. We had time together in Hawaii. That sunset on the beach?" Even as the words left her mouth, Nicole knew deep down what that sunset had really been like: forty minutes of reshooting the same pose until their smiles felt painted on, the romance long dead before they got that one shot. "You used to support my dreams," she finished weakly, and instantly regretted it.

"Yeah," Jen said coolly. "And you used to support mine. Earlier, when I was riding, actually enjoying something for the first time in months? All I could think about was how you'd want me to pose. It ruined the whole experience." She walked out, leaving Nicole standing in the kitchen, surrounded by strangers who'd witnessed their moment of unfiltered reality.

The chef and waitress had turned back to their work,

but Nicole caught the dark-haired waitress sneaking glances at her. That earlier admiration was now tinged with something else. Pity?

Nicole felt exposed, raw. The weight of strangers witnessing their private pain made her skin crawl.

She straightened her shoulders and adjusted her hat, then pulled her phone from her pocket.

"Just got the most amazing riding shots of Jen," she typed. "Can't wait to share! Living that ranch life. #blessed 🐎💚 " Her thumb hovered over 'post'. Through the open door, she saw Melissa by the ring, already talking to another couple. Already moving on to the next opportunity, the next connection, the next rung on the endless ladder they were climbing.

The yacht invitation was a lifeline. A chance to fix everything. Or break it completely.

She hit 'post.'

Chapter Seven

The lull between lunch and dinner service found Ana seeking refuge in the walk-in refrigerator, using the inventory as an excuse to catch her breath and steal a moment of quiet. Her borrowed shirt clung to her damp back, and her feet throbbed.

Through the clouded glass door, Dani's voice called out above the clatter of prep work. "Where's the cilantro? Ana? You see it in there?"

"Checking!" Ana called back, but her gaze was fixed on her phone, scrolling through Nicole's latest post. The photos were breathtaking—Jen on horseback, sunlight haloing her hair, her smile... different, somehow. More genuine. The caption, however, made Ana's stomach twist: "Living that ranch life with my love. #KingRanch #sapphiclove #couplegoals🩶"

She'd witnessed the reality behind those photos. How Jen had walked away, leaving Nicole looking uncharacteristically lost and vulnerable.

The walk-in door swung open. "Seriously, Ana, where's the cilantro?"

Ana jumped, nearly dropping her phone. Dani stood in the doorway, backlit by the kitchen lights, her chef's blacks bearing the marks of a long day's work.

"I was just—"

"Stalking their Instagram again?" Dani asked, her voice gentle despite the words. She stepped inside, letting the door swing shut.

"It wasn't like that," Ana said, struggling to articulate the mix of emotions swirling within her. "The photos are beautiful, but..."

"The photos are deceiving, *mi amor*." Dani moved closer, her presence a comforting warmth in the chilled air. "You saw how they were earlier."

"Everyone fights."

"Not like that," Dani said softly. "Not with so much..."

"Pain? Resentment?" Ana offered, remembering the hurt in Nicole's eyes.

"Yeah."

They stood in silence, surrounded by crates of produce and herbs.

"You know what the worst part is?" Ana said finally. "I still want a small slice of their life. Even after seeing..." She gestured vaguely. "All of that."

"The cracks?"

"Yeah," Ana said, looking down at her phone, at the carefully curated images. "Is that crazy?"

Dani was quiet for a long moment, then asked, "Remember last month? When the radiator broke?"

Ana nodded. Their apartment had been frigid for three days while they scraped together the money for repairs.

"Remember what we did?"

A smile touched Ana's lips. "We built a blanket fort,

strung up all the Christmas lights, made hot chocolate, and watched movies." Her grin widened. "And had great sex."

Dani shot her a smirk, a faint blush rising to her cheeks. "And?"

"I loved it." The memory warmed Ana. "Despite the cold. Despite everything."

"Exactly." Dani's arms slipped around her waist. "That's real life, baby. Not this..." She nodded toward the phone. "This performance."

Before Ana could respond, the walk-in door swung open again. "There you are! Stop smooching and get to work." Mike's voice shattered the intimate moment. "Dinner prep starts in ten."

Ana straightened herself, hiding her phone behind her back. "We weren't smooching, we were—"

"Sure, sure. And I wasn't flirting with the produce guy this morning." Mike rolled his eyes, but a smile tugged at his lips. "But since you've managed not to drop anything yet, I'll let it slide. Now move your butts—these influencers aren't going to feed themselves. Well, actually, they might not eat much anyway, but you know what I mean." He pointed to the kitchen. "Dani, you're on mains tonight. And you... What was your name again?"

"Ana"

"Right. Ana. You keep this up tonight—you know, not destroying my reputation or dropping soup on anyone—and you can come back. Work with Dani on the regular, if you want."

"Really?" Ana's face lit up. "That would be amazing. I'd love that."

"Save the grateful for your wedding vows or whatever," Mike said, waving a hand dismissively. "Just do your job.

The lesbian couple—they're in the east garden. I need someone to bring them water. You've been good with them all day, so take care of it."

As Mike disappeared back into the kitchen, Ana turned to Dani, lowering her voice. "Do you think he means it? About letting me come back?"

"Oh yeah." Dani smiled. "Mike's like that. Once he decides he likes you, you're in. And look at me, getting put on mains—you must be my lucky charm today." She re-tied her apron strings. "Think about it. We could actually work the same shifts."

"No more missing each other?" Ana asked, her voice soft. "No more me crawling into bed when you're crawling out?"

"No more cold sheets," Dani said, stepping closer. "No more trying to guess if you've eaten, or if I should leave you dinner."

Ana's eyes widened with excitement. "We could actually have breakfast together. Like, sitting down, not just me watching you rush out the door."

"Mm. And I wouldn't have to worry about waking you up when you've just gotten to sleep." Dani's eyes crinkled at the corners. "Though I kind of like how grumpy you look in the morning, all wrapped up in blankets like a burrito."

"I'm not grumpy," Ana protested, but she was smiling. "I just... appreciate silence."

"And maybe you could finally come to one of my softball games."

"God, yes," Ana said, touching Dani's arm. "I'd love that. Though I might be a terrible cheerleader—I still don't really get the rules."

"That's okay. You can just sit there and look pretty. Maybe bring me water between innings." Dani smirked. "I promise I'll actually drink it instead of just posing with it." She stepped back with a wink. "Now get going before Mike comes back. And Ana?" She waited until Ana turned back. "You're already better at this than most people he hires. You've got this."

Chapter Eight

Balancing the water tray, Ana followed the sound of raised voices, the crushed shell path crunching softly beneath her shoes. The ranch's patio area, constructed of limestone and weathered wooden beams, was surrounded by native plants—agave and yucca rising from beds of crushed granite.

She heard them before she saw them.

"I just need you to understand," Nicole's voice, strained, carried from behind a massive live oak. "This yacht trip could change everything."

"Yeah?" Jen's laugh was harsh, devoid of humor. "Like this ranch was supposed to change everything? Like that sponsored wedding shoot changed everything?"

Ana slowed, her heart pounding. She should announce her presence, but her feet felt rooted to the spot.

"The bills aren't going to pay themselves," Nicole said. "The mortgage—"

"Then maybe we should sell the house. Sell the cars. Sell all of it."

"We can't! Everyone expects—"

"Fuck everyone!"

The outburst startled a flock of grackles from the oak's branches. Ana jumped, liquid sloshing in the glasses. The movement must have made a sound, because Nicole suddenly appeared from around the trunk.

"Oh," she said, visibly composing herself. "Water. Yes. Thank you."

Ana stepped forward, acutely aware of her every movement. Jen stood rigidly by a cluster of native lantana, her back turned.

"Here," Ana said softly, holding out the tray. "I brought some lemonade, too, if you prefer."

"Thank you." Nicole took a glass, her fingers trembling slightly. A drop of lemonade splashed onto her pristine white top. "Shit," she muttered, then caught herself. "Sorry. I mean—"

"I have a stain stick in the car," Ana offered. "If you want..."

Nicole looked at her then, really looked at her, for perhaps the first time all day. "That's... that's very kind."

"Don't bother," Jen said, her voice flat. "It's not like she can post in a stained shirt anyway. Anything less than perfect is unacceptable to Nicole."

"Jen, please—"

"I'm done." Jen turned, and the raw pain in her eyes struck Ana. "With all of it. The posing, the pretending, the —" She gestured at the ranch grounds. "This isn't us anymore, Nic. I don't even know who we are."

She walked away, leaving Nicole alone with her lemonade, her stained shirt, and her crumbling world.

Ana stood frozen, unsure of her next move. Leave? Stay? Offer the stain stick again?

"She'll calm down," Nicole said, more to herself than to

Ana. "She always does. I just need to..." She pulled out her phone, fingers moving automatically. "Maybe if I post about the sunset... or the live oaks..."

Her voice cracked on the last word, and the phone slipped from her grasp, clattering to the ground. As she bent to retrieve it, she burst into tears.

Nicole crumpled, her designer jeans hitting the shell path, her shoulders shaking with silent sobs.

For a moment, Ana stood frozen, tray still in hand, caught between her instinct to help and her professional boundaries. But something in Nicole's broken posture decided for her. She'd seen this kind of breakdown before—in the nursing home, in the ER during her clinical rotations. Different circumstances, but the same pain.

She set the tray on a nearby bench and knelt beside Nicole, close enough to offer support, but without touching her. Nicole's body shook with ragged breaths, her face hidden in her hands, mascara staining her fingers.

"I can't," she whispered between sobs. "I can't keep... I don't know how to fix it."

Ana said nothing, knowing that sometimes silence was the kindest response. The giant live oak creaked above them, its wintergreen leaves rustling in the cold Texas wind. In the distance, a horse whinnied. Somewhere closer, boots crunched on the path—staff members going about their duties, pretending not to notice.

"Is there anything I can do?" Ana finally asked, placing a hand on Nicole's shoulder.

Nicole just shook her head, still hiding behind her hands. Her breathing was becoming erratic, verging on hyperventilation. The January chill was seeping through their clothes, and Ana could see goosebumps rising on Nicole's bare arms.

"Here," she said gently. "Let's get you up. It's too cold to sit on the ground." She offered her hand, the same way she did for Mrs. Rodriguez when helping her from her bed. Nicole took it, her grip desperate.

They rose together, Nicole swaying slightly. Ana guided her to the bench, positioning her away from the main path, offering what privacy she could. Nicole's breathing gradually steadied, though tears still streaked her face.

"I'm sorry," Nicole said finally, wiping at her eyes. Then, as if someone had flipped a switch, she straightened. Her hands moved automatically to smooth her hair, adjust her clothes, rebuild her facade. "God, I'm so sorry. You shouldn't have had to... This isn't..." She took a deep breath, and Ana watched in amazement as the influencer persona slid back into place like a mask. "Thank you. For your kindness. And the stain stick offer." She attempted a smile. "Though I guess it's a little late for that now."

"It's okay," Ana said, taking a step back, understanding that the moment was over. "I have make-up wipes in the car too, if you need some."

"No, no." Nicole was already reaching for her phone again, her fingers hovering over the screen like a lifeline. "I'm fine. Really. I just need a minute to..."

She didn't finish the sentence, but she didn't need to. Ana recognized the desperate need to pretend everything was normal, to keep going as if nothing had happened. She'd seen it countless times in her patients, in their families. Sometimes the only way forward was to act as if you weren't breaking apart.

"Of course," Ana said, picking up the tray. "Take care." She turned to leave, but Nicole's voice stopped her.

"Could you... could you not mention this to anyone?"

"Of course not," Ana said, understanding that 'anyone' meant more than just the other staff or guests.

"Thank you." Nicole got up and gestured toward the house. "I'd better go freshen up. The light's fading anyway. Can't waste golden hour."

Ana stood alone in the gathering dusk. She could see the staff parking lot where Dani's old Civic sat nestled among ranch trucks and catering vans. Their dented, beloved car, with its perpetually broken AC, a constant reminder of their own imperfect reality.

The dinner service bell rang, summoning her back to work. As she walked back to the kitchen, her phone buzzed in her pocket. A new post from Nicole:

"Sunset magic under century-old oaks with my love. Living for these moments. #blessed #ranchlife #KingRanch #Texas 🐨 🐴"

The photo was flawless—Nicole and Jen, bathed in the golden light of the setting sun, the tree creating a dreamy frame.

Both smiling. Both radiant. Both lying.

Chapter Nine

Nicole sat alone in the darkness on the limestone steps of the main house, her phone clutched in her lap. Inside, the other influencers were finishing dinner. She could hear their laughter, and a familiar sense of anxiety twisted in her stomach. She should be in there, networking. Instead, she was hiding.

Jen hadn't come to dinner.

A message from Melissa lit up her screen: "Nicole, you're missing out on the cocktails! And I need your answer about the yacht."

Nicole let the message fade without responding. Another immediately took its place: 'Those sunset photos are performing amazingly! See what happens when you lean into authenticity?'

Authenticity. The word felt hollow, devoid of meaning.

She opened her camera roll, scrolling through the day's photos. The breakfast shoot from that morning—poached eggs and salmon, followed with avocado toast, compote topped with edible flowers. Steam rising artfully from their coffee mugs, the King Ranch logo prominent in the shot.

The riding photos came next. Her own shots were great—she'd spent an hour getting them right. One of Nicole astride the dappled mare, her body positioned just so, the morning light catching her hair beneath the Stetson. Her boot positioned perfectly in the stirrup, her profile captured at the exact angle that highlighted her cheekbones. Another of her looking thoughtfully into the distance, one hand resting loosely on the reins, the horse's neck arched elegantly. She'd even managed to catch the moment when the horse had tossed its head, creating a sense of wild energy while Nicole remained serenely in control. Everything about the photos screamed "natural horsewoman"—never mind that she'd needed help mounting and had barely moved from that spot once she was up.

Then came the ones of Jen on horseback, captioned "Living her best ranch life!" Nicole remembered the tight set of Jen's jaw, how she'd snapped, "Are we done yet? I just want to go for a ride."

Movement caught Nicole's eye. It was that waitress again, the one who'd witnessed their fight and her breakdown. She was crossing the parking lot with her girlfriend, the chef. They walked close, shoulders touching, their laughter light and easy. The chef gestured animatedly, nearly dropping her car keys. The waitress caught them, their hands lingering for a moment.

Nicole watched them, unable to look away. The chef whispered something in the waitress's ear, making her laugh and swat playfully at her arm. No posing, no forced smiles, just... genuine affection.

The scene triggered a memory, so vivid it hurt. Jen in their old apartment's tiny kitchen, attempting to recreate some fancy pasta recipe she'd found. Jen, wearing Nicole's old college T-shirt, was already dusted with flour when

Nicole came up behind her to "help." She'd managed to knock over the entire bag of flour, creating a white mushroom cloud that coated everything—including their faces and hair. They'd ended up splitting a package of Oreos for dinner, still finding flour in the most unlikely places days later.

Nicole couldn't remember the last time they'd cooked together. Their new kitchen, with its marble countertops and designer appliances, was more of a set than a living space, every meal an opportunity for content—plated, styled, but rarely enjoyed.

She swallowed hard. When was the last time she and Jen had shared a laugh like that one? A genuine laugh, not the camera-ready chuckle they'd honed to perfection for their followers.

The memory sparked another, older one. Fresh out of college, she was sitting at a drab cubicle in a marketing firm, staring at a spreadsheet filled with someone else's data. She was a cog in a machine, her creativity stifled, her days measured in billable hours. Jen, ever supportive, had listened to her nightly complaints, her hand warm on Nicole's back as she vented.

"You're meant for more than this," Jen had said one evening, her eyes full of belief. "You're so creative, so full of life. You should be doing something that makes you shine."

Nicole had scoffed, gesturing around their tiny apartment. "Like what? We need money, Jen. Stability." "We have each other," Jen had replied, her voice firm. "That's all we need. We'll make it work."

That's when she'd started experimenting with photography, taking pictures of their everyday life—their cat, their meals, their weekend adventures. It was a way to break the frustration and boredom of her job. She'd discovered a knack for styling and a passion for capturing beauty in the mundane. When she started posting her photos online, the response had been immediate and overwhelming. People connected with her aesthetic, her eye for detail, her ability to make even a simple cup of coffee look like a work of art.

The followers came quickly, then the brands. It had felt like validation, proof that she was more than just a number cruncher in a corporate box, that she had something special to offer. And when the first paycheck arrived, enough to cover their rent for the month, it had felt like a miracle. Like Jen had been right all along.

Nicole hadn't set out to become an influencer. She'd just wanted to share her creativity, to connect with others, to build a more meaningful life. And somewhere along the way, she'd lost sight of that original goal. The pursuit of likes and followers had become an end in itself, and the pressure to maintain their carefully constructed image had driven a wedge between her and the woman who had believed in her before anyone else.

"There you are."

Nicole's heart gave a startled jump. But it was just Melissa, a martini glass in hand, her heels clicking against the limestone—completely impractical for a ranch, but apparently Melissa never let practicality interfere with her image.

"We're moving to the fire pit for a nightcap." Melissa settled beside her, the wool of her cape brushing Nicole's arm. "And we need to discuss the yacht. I can't keep the invitation open forever. By the way, where's Jen?"

"I haven't..." Nicole cleared her throat. "Jen's not feeling well. She's sleeping, but I'll check with her when she wakes up."

"Listen, babe." Melissa's voice sharpened, losing its

sugary tone. "This isn't just any yacht trip. This is the *Pacific Dream*." She leaned closer, her perfume cutting through the clean ranch air. "And between us? Your numbers have been slipping lately. I've noticed, and so have the brands."

A stab of anxiety came with the mention of her metrics, but Nicole was too emotionally drained to mount a defense. Through the parking lot shadows, she watched the waitress and the chef drive away, the brake lights disappearing down the ranch road, swallowed by the vast Texas night. Above her, the stars wheeled in their ancient, indifferent patterns, oblivious to hashtags, follower counts and hearts breaking.

"She hates it," she whispered, the words escaping like a confession. "All of it."

"Then she needs to grow up," Melissa said, her voice carrying the same practiced authority she used in her 'girl boss mindset' posts. "This is your career. Your future. If she can't support that..." She tapped her nails against her glass. "You know, lots of influencer couples break up. Some, like me, even gained followers from it. Just saying."

Nicole frowned and turned to her. The casual way Melissa talked about leveraging heartbreak for followers made her stomach turn. "It's not like that with us," she said. "Jen and I... we're good. We're the real deal."

"Are you?" Melissa's tone was almost pitying.

"Yes." Nicole sat up straighter, finding a fragment of strength. "We'll be there. Count us in." The words tasted bitter even as she said them, and shame crept up her neck. She should be defending Jen more strongly, not volunteering her for something she knew would make her miserable.

"Excellent." Melissa rose to her feet. "I'm looking

forward to hosting you." She paused, her shadow falling across Nicole. "With or without Jen."

Nicole sat alone long after Melissa's footsteps had faded away. The night air carried the scent of cedar and dust, so different from the artificial vanilla of their home diffusers. A coyote called in the distance, answered by another.

She thought of the waitress catching her girlfriend's keys, their genuine laughter echoing in the parking lot. Her phone felt heavy in her hand. She should post something—maintain engagement, keep the algorithm happy. Instead, she scrolled and stared at a photo from three years ago, one she'd never shared: Jen asleep on their old couch, drooling slightly, their ancient cat who was still alive back then sprawled across her chest.

Jen was right. They'd been so happy in that cramped apartment, just the two of them and their dreams. They'd spent their evenings watching bad reality TV and sharing leftover Chinese food, and somehow that had been enough. She remembered how Jen would fall asleep halfway through every movie, no matter how early they started it, and how they'd leave the Christmas lights up all year because she loved them. Everything had been so simple then, and she missed them—not the apartment or the cheap takeout or even the Christmas lights, but *them*.

Chapter Ten

The kitchen was finally quiet, save for the hum of the industrial dishwasher running its final cycle. Ana wiped down the stainless steel prep station, her borrowed white shirt wrinkled and stained, her feet aching from hours of service.

"Here, let me help with that." She moved to assist Marco, the young kitchen porter who was struggling with a stack of heavy serving platters. "These things are awkward."

"Thanks," he mumbled, clearly exhausted. "Influencers use twice as many dishes as normal people. All those setups for photos..."

"Tell me about it." Ana carefully placed the platters in their racks. "I must have reset that dessert table four times just so they could get the right shots."

Through the window, she could see them still at it, snapping pictures of their cocktails by the fire pit. Nicole and Jen weren't there.

"You coming?" Dani appeared beside her, changed back into her regular clothes, car keys dangling from her finger. "Or are you planning to stare at them all night?"

Ana turned, taking in her girlfriend's tired eyes, a dust of flour still on her cheek. She was real and present and here, and God, she loved her.

"Do you think they're okay?"

"Who?"

"Nicole and Jen."

Dani sighed. "Baby..."

"I know, I know. It's none of my business." Ana untied her apron. "It's just... that fight. And then Jen missing dinner... And earlier, when Nicole was crying—"

"Baby, you're worried about strangers who don't even know your name."

"They're not—" Ana stopped, catching herself. But they weren't strangers, were they? She knew their morning routine, their favorite foods, she knew their home inside out. Except... "I guess they are."

Dani stepped closer, taking Ana's hands in hers. "What's really bothering you?"

Ana looked down at their intertwined fingers - Dani's callused from years of kitchen work, her own marked with tiny bruises and cuts from nursing home care. Not a manicure between them.

"They looked so perfect online," she said finally. "Like they had it all figured out. I'd see their posts and think... maybe we'll have that someday, you know?"

"And now?"

Ana turned away from the window, facing Dani fully. In the harsh kitchen lights, she could see every line of exhaustion on her girlfriend's face, every streak of flour in her hair, every mark of a long day's honest work.

"Now I want a buffet in bed," she said. "With you."

Dani's smile was slow, radiant, just for her. "Yeah?"

"Yeah." Ana leaned in, pressing her forehead to Dani's.

"I'll plate it really pretty for you." She pointed to the large paper bag Dani had packed. "So, what's for dinner?"

Dani grinned. "For starters, we've got fresh bread, some of that fancy smoked salmon, and—because my girlfriend is basically a mouse—an obscene amount of cheese."

"How obscene?" Ana peered into the bag.

"Three kinds. And look—" Dani pulled out a small container. "Pomegranate seeds. To make it extra bougie for my Instagram-loving baby."

"Shut up," Ana laughed. "What else?"

"Main course: dauphinoise potatoes, those steamed vegetables, and two beautiful steaks. Couldn't save any sauce, but I got some garlic butter to melt on top."

"You're the best girlfriend in the whole entire universe," Ana said, wrapping her arms around Dani's waist. "Like, the absolute bestest." She batted her eyelashes. "Dare I ask if you have dessert too?"

Dani licked her lips, leaning closer. "Baby, I'm your dessert."

Ana nudged her playfully. "You're ridiculous."

"Fine, fine. I also packed chocolate mousse."

"God, I love you." Ana shrieked with excitement, then pulled her in for a kiss. "And for the record," she mumbled against Dani's lips. "I will have you for dessert."

"Mmm..." Dani arched a brow. "And maybe we could have a shower together? I look like I've been in a fight with a flour sack."

"And lost," Ana agreed, brushing some flour from Dani's face. "Badly."

They said their goodbyes to the remaining staff, Marco giving them a tired wave as he finished mopping. Mike appeared just as they were leaving.

"Good work today, both of you," he called after them.

"Ana, don't forget—you're on the schedule for next weekend."

"Thanks, Mike! I'll see you Saturday."

Ana was practically skipping as they pushed through the heavy kitchen doors into the cool night air. Her feet were sore and her back ached from twelve hours of carrying trays, but her heart felt light. She'd spent the whole day stealing glances at Dani in the kitchen, sharing secret smiles between services, working in sync. And now there would be more days like this—long and exhausting and wonderful, traveling together, working together, falling into bed together...

Their old Civic waited in the staff lot, far from the luxury cars clustered near the main house. Dani was humming something under her breath; she always did that when she was in a good mood.

"I can't believe you got put on mains," Ana said, bumping her shoulder. "My girlfriend, moving up in the world."

"All thanks to my good luck charm." The keys slipped from Dani's fingers as she fumbled with them. Ana caught them mid-fall, and their hands met. For a moment, they just stood there, fingers intertwined around the keys.

"Nice catch," Dani murmured, pulling Ana a little closer. "Good reflexes."

Ana laughed. "Why are you so sexy today?" There was something unexpectedly hot about working with Dani, about watching her command her kitchen.

"You think I'm sexy?"

"Uh-huh. I've been watching you today. I love how you move with such confidence between stations. And I love how you roll up your sleeves, revealing the muscles in your forearms." Ana stroked Dani's arm and squeezed it. "And I love how you brush your hair back with the back of your wrist when your hands are full. Even now, dishevelled after a long day, you're still the sexiest thing I've ever seen."

Dani threw her head back and laughed, then wedged Ana between herself and the car. "Damn, if I'd known you got this hot and bothered watching me work, I would've brought you to the kitchen ages ago." She brushed her thumb over Ana's bottom lip. "And here I thought you only had eyes for Nicole and Jen."

"Guess you'll have to keep me around to find out," Ana murmured, sliding her hands around Dani's hips.

"As much as I'd love to continue this conversation," Dani said, reluctantly stepping back, "if we don't get in this car now, we might never make it home. And I've got plans for you that definitely require a bed."

They untangled themselves and got in the car, both a little breathless. The heater rattled to life, fighting against the January chill.

As Dani drove them home, Ana's phone lit up with a notification. Nicole's latest post: "Dinner with our ranch family! Living for these moments! #blessed #ranchlife #KingRanch #Texas 🤠 🤍"

It was a selfie of Nicole with the other influencers gathered around her, all smiles and poses. But Jen wasn't in it.

She turned off her notifications, slipped her phone in her pocket, and reached for Dani's hand across the console. Some things, she was learning, were better left unfiltered.

Chapter Eleven

An unsettling silence greeted Nicole as she unlocked the door to their Calabasas house. Her footsteps echoed on the marble floors, a lonely sound in the cavernous space. After the three-hour flight from Texas and the drive from LAX, she felt drained, hollow. The day at King Ranch had been a blur of increasingly forced excuses about Jen's absence.

"Just a work emergency," she'd told Melissa over breakfast, the lie tasting bitter on her tongue.

The memory made Nicole's stomach turn. She'd spent the afternoon in their luxury suite, going through the motions. Pretending to soak in the oversized copper tub, her arm stiff from holding her selfie-stick.

Now, standing in the empty foyer, Nicole felt the overwhelming urge to take a real bath, to wash away the day's pretense. But first, she needed to find Jen.

"Jen?" she called out. No answer.

Nicole moved through their spacious home, each room more beautiful and more achingly empty than the last. The silence was oppressive. Had their house always been this quiet? This hollow?

Their bedroom was unnaturally tidy - expensive linens perfectly smooth, throw pillows meticulously arranged. Nicole stared down at the bed. When was the last time they'd actually spent a lazy morning here, just stayed in bed for no reason?

"Jen?" Nicole called out again, louder this time. The answering silence made her chest tighten. "Jen!" Her heart began to race as a terrible thought struck her. She yanked open the wardrobe door, her hands shaking.

Jen's clothes were still there, but something felt off. Nicole's breath came in short gasps as she frantically pushed through the hangers. The old UCLA hoodie was missing—the one Jen wore every day after work, the one she'd 'borrowed' from Nicole during their first year together.

Nicole spun around, her vision blurring. "JEN!" Her voice cracked with rising panic. "JENNIFER!"

The master bath was empty. No sign of Jen's practical drugstore products among Nicole's collection of expensive creams and serums. Had she packed them for the ranch? She honestly couldn't remember.

Panic rose like a tide, threatening to drown her. Nicole ran back downstairs. The coffee maker was cold and empty, Jen's favorite mug absent from the dishwasher. She hadn't even had a coffee when she got home.

"JEN!" The scream tore from her throat, raw and desperate. "JENNIFER!" She couldn't breathe, couldn't think past the crushing fear that Jen was gone, that she'd finally had enough.

Tears streamed down her face as she sank to the floor, pressing her forehead to her knees, gasping for air.

"Nicole?" Jen's concerned voice, came from the doorway. "Babe, what's wrong?"

Nicole's head snapped up. Through her tears, she saw Jen standing there in her work clothes—dirt on her knees, hair ruffled—looking bewildered and concerned.

"Oh my god." Nicole scrambled to her feet, but her legs felt like jelly. She half-crawled, half-stumbled toward Jen, who met her halfway, catching her in her arms.

"Hey, hey, what happened?" Jen's voice was soft as she pulled her close. She smelled of soil, sweat, and that generic shampoo she refused to give up—everything Nicole needed right now. "I'm right here. I've got you."

"I thought—" Nicole's voice broke. "Your hoodie was gone, your mug... I thought—"

"Hey, hey." Jen's arms came around her, strong and sure. "I'm right here. I just went to work on the Peterson's garden. Needed to clear my head." She pulled back slightly, studying Nicole's face. "The hoodie's in the laundry, and I took my mug to the job site."

"I thought you'd left me."

Jen was quiet for a moment, her hand moving in slow circles on Nicole's back. "I thought about it," she said finally. "Been thinking about it a lot lately."

Nicole's heart clenched. "Jen—"

"Let me finish." Jen's arms tightened around her. "I thought about leaving, maybe staying with my sister for a while. But then I realized something."

"What?" Nicole barely dared to breathe.

"That I don't want to leave you. I want to leave *this*." Jen gestured at their house. "All of it." She touched Nicole's face, wiping away tears Nicole hadn't realized were falling. "I want us back. The real us."

"I don't know how," Nicole admitted. "Everything's so tangled up now. The mortgage, the cars—"

"We'll sell the house," Jen said. "And then we'll take it from there." She smiled, a real smile that made Nicole's heart ache. "I'll come on the yacht trip."

Nicole pulled back slightly, surprised. "You will?"

"Yes." Jen tucked a strand of hair behind Nicole's ear. "Until we sell the house, we still need to keep up with the payments. So yes, I'll come on the yacht trip. But only if you agree to sell the house."

Nicole looked around their kitchen—the marble countertops she'd insisted on, the designer appliances they rarely used, the custom lighting she'd had installed for photos. This house had been everything she'd ever wanted. Or thought she wanted. But lately, every corner of it felt heavy with obligation. The mortgage payments were always on her mind and the showroom surfaces demanded constant upkeep for appearance sake.

"Okay," she said, and as soon as the word left her mouth, she felt lighter. "Let's sell it."

"Thank you," Jen whispered, studying Nicole's face for any sign of doubt. "I want you to have the career you want, babe. If being an influencer is your dream, I'll support that. But I need to focus on my own work too. When things are normal again, when we're not drowning in debt... I just can't be part of the content creation anymore. That's not my dream. It never was."

"I know," Nicole said, wrapping her arms tighter around Jen's waist. "I'm sorry I kept pushing you into it." She wiped at her eyes and sniffed. "And I appreciate that you're coming on that trip with me. It will be the last time, I promise."

Jen's mouth quirked into a half-smile. "Three days of

pretending to love sailing with Melissa St. Clair isn't exactly my idea of fun, but if it helps to pay the bills..." She shrugged. "But I need one more thing."

"Anything."

"When we're together—like at the end of the day, or when we're having dinner, or when we're in bed—I need you present," Jen said. "During the day, when you're working, be on your phone all you want. That's your job, I get it. But when it's our time..." She cupped Nicole's face in her hands. "I want you. Just you. No phones in bed, no checking notifications. Deal?"

Nicole buried her face in Jen's neck, breathing in her scent. The panic from earlier still echoed in her chest—that gut-wrenching moment when she'd thought Jen was gone. "Deal," she whispered against Jen's skin. "Just don't leave me."

Chapter Twelve

Ana woke before her alarm, disoriented. After years of night shifts, her body still expected darkness, but the sun was rising, and there was Dani, still asleep beside her.

The past week had been a blur. She and Dani had worked at Garcia's for three consecutive days, which was immediately followed by two brutal night shifts at the nursing home. There, Mr. Jones, one of her favorite patients, had taken a turn for the worse. His dementia had spiraled, leaving him confused and terrified, lashing out at shadows only he could see. She'd found him at 3:00 a.m., tangled in his sheets, fighting invisible enemies.

"They're coming," he'd screamed, his skeletal hands clawing at the air. "Tommy! We have to move! They're coming!"

It had taken Ana hours to calm him, to coax him back from Vietnam and the memories that haunted him. She'd held his trembling hands, speaking softly, constantly, until her throat was raw. "You're safe, Mr. Jones. You're in Paradise Valley. Tommy's not here, but I am. I've got you."

She was tired, her muscles aching from lifting plates and patients, from dancing around other servers and maneuvering medical equipment. But it was a good kind of tired, and she was happy with the direction her life was moving.

Today was going to be good—they both had the day off, something that hadn't happened in... she couldn't even remember how long. Between her night shifts at Paradise Valley and Dani's endless hours at Garcia's, their lives had become a complicated dance of hello-goodbye kisses and hastily scrawled notes. But today... today was just for them, and apart from Dani's softball game, they had no plans.

The thought made her giddy. They could do anything—or nothing at all. Maybe they'd finally check out that new food truck down the block or binge-watch the series they'd started months ago.

Her phone buzzed on the nightstand. Ana's hand moved toward it automatically, but she stopped herself. Instead, she rolled over and pressed a kiss to Dani's shoulder.

"Mmm," Dani mumbled, still mostly asleep. "What time is it?"

"Early," Ana whispered. "But I'm wide awake. I'm so excited to have the day off with you."

Dani stretched, becoming more alert. "Then let me make you breakfast. I brought home some stuff from last night's wedding—those fancy little potatoes we served with the beef tenderloin, some caramelized onions, even managed to snag a few strips of that expensive bacon they barely touched." She propped herself up on one elbow, grinning. "I'm thinking breakfast hash with a fried egg on top. Maybe those little cherry tomatoes too, if they're still good."

"I won't say no to that, chef." Ana grinned and inched

closer, brushing her lips against Dani's. "A real gourmet breakfast and the day off?"

"Perks of being a chef." Dani stretched, her old Selena T-shirt riding up. She pulled Ana close, and Ana settled into the familiar curves of her girlfriend's body. "I didn't see you yesterday. How was work?"

Ana leaned her head against Dani's neck, letting out a long breath. "Hard. Mr. Jones kept thinking he was back in Vietnam. Kept calling out for his brother." She felt Dani's arms tighten around her. "He was so scared, Dani. And nothing I did seemed enough. Sometimes I wonder if I'm really helping or just... just watching them slip away."

"Baby," Dani said, stroking her cheek. "You help. Every day, every shift. You remember their stories, their families. You make them feel seen."

"I just... I don't want to leave them completely, you know? Even with the Garcia's job. They need me."

Dani's fingers combed through Ana's hair. "That's why you're only cutting back to two nights. Because you've got the biggest heart of anyone I know. But you need a life too."

"I know. And the occasional day off with you." Ana pressed a kiss to Dani's lips and slid out of bed. "Stay there. I'll be back with coffee."

When she turned on the coffee maker, it made an alarming gurgling sound and started smoking slightly.

"Shit," Ana turned it off, then back on again. It seemed to do the job.

"Need help?"

"No, I've got it. Just... maybe we should start saving for a new one? Add it to the list?"

"The list" had started as a joke—all the things they'd buy when they could afford them. A coffee maker that didn't require mechanical intervention to function. A bed frame to get their mattress off the floor. Maybe even a bigger apartment, one where they didn't have to choose between a dining table and a wardrobe. But now, with Ana's new job at Garcia's...

"I did the math," Ana said, grabbing mugs and adding sugar to them. "With the extra shifts at Garcia's, even cutting back at Paradise Valley... we could maybe start looking. For a better place."

"Yeah?" Dani called from the bed.

"Nothing fancy," Ana added quickly. "Just... maybe somewhere with a real kitchen? Where you could actually try out those recipes you're always talking about?"

"And maybe a separate bedroom with enough space for an actual dresser?" Dani quipped. "Don't get me wrong; I like the smell of coffee in bed. But the smell of garlic on the sheets... not so much."

"How about a bathtub?" Ana dared to dream.

"Whoa there, princess," Dani laughed. "Let's start with the coffee maker. Baby steps."

Ana added coffee and milk to the mugs, stirred them, and carefully made her way back to bed. The whole day stretched ahead of them, full of possibility. She couldn't stop smiling.

Her phone buzzed on the nightstand as she set down the coffee, and she picked it up, already suspecting what the notification was for. Nicole had posted a series of photos: first, her holding up a navy-and-white-striped top in their beautiful bedroom, then artistic shots of a half-packed suitcase. In the background, Ana could see a silver tray holding what looked like fresh mint tea and an expensive jar of honey, surrounded by plump dates. "Packing for our Valentine's cruise," the caption read. "Can't wait to have some quality time with my one."

"You got that look again," Dani said, glancing at her screen.

"What look?"

"Like you're worried about strangers." Dani smiled softly. "They'll figure it out. Or they won't. Not your circus, not your monkeys."

"Hmm…" Ana put her phone down. "Hey, speaking of circus—you have a game today, right?"

"I do. Are you coming to cheer me on?"

"You bet." Ana grinned. "I'm so excited. First, that fancy breakfast you promised me, and then I get to watch my girl hit home runs—"

"They're called runs in softball, baby."

"Whatever. I'll learn." Ana shifted closer, trailing her fingers along Dani's arm. "And then after the game…" her voice trailed off, and she arched an eyebrow suggestively.

"After the game?" Dani looked her over and licked her lips. "That's an awful long time to wait…" She rolled on top of Ana, pinning her to the mattress, their coffee forgotten. "Why not right now?"

Chapter Thirteen

The *Pacific Dream*, with its clean lines and modern luxury, cut through the waters off Marina del Rey. Glass, polished teak, and chrome railings gleamed despite the overcast February sky. Just hours ago, they'd boarded, welcomed by staff in crisp white uniforms who offered them plush slippers and mimosas in crystal flutes.

Even Nicole, used to the trappings of influence, had felt small stepping onto that deck. She'd watched Jen's face carefully, noting how her girlfriend's jaw had tightened at the ostentation of it all—the fresh orchids in every corner, the casual display of wealth. *You're lucky to be here,* she'd reminded herself as they were led to their cabin. *People would kill for this opportunity.* The thought had echoed again during lunch, served on the upper deck under elegant heating lamps that fought against the February chill. She'd watched the other couples. A guest list comprising of Melissa's influencer "friends," and Nicole tried to ignore the fact that she and Jen were clearly here to fill the diversity quota.

Since boarding, Jen had been quiet, speaking only when necessary. She'd disappeared below deck almost immediately after the welcome lunch, muttering something about unpacking.

The memory of lunch made Nicole uneasy. She'd watched Jen push her fork through the butter-poached lobster, barely touching the caviar-dotted blinis and truffle-infused risotto. Each dish had been more extravagant than the last, designed to be photographed more than eaten.

Jen wasn't comfortable in this setting, but she was trying, and Nicole was grateful for that. She'd made polite small talk, complimented Melissa on her yacht, and posed for pictures.

The seating hadn't been accidental—nothing on this yacht was. Melissa had placed herself at the head of the glass-topped table, Charlotte Ming and her husband flanking her like bookends. The Weber twins held court halfway down, their laughs carrying across the Veuve Clicquot being poured into endless crystal glasses.

And then there was Harper, who had somehow ended up next to Jen. Even now, Nicole could picture how Harper had leaned forward, chin resting on her hand, feigning fascination at Jen's description of California-native plants.

Nicole tugged at her white tailored jacket, adjusting how it fell over the silk top underneath. She'd chosen this outfit carefully—the palazzo pants giving an effortless elegance, the plunging neckline of her top adding just the right amount of allure while still keeping it classy. Her silver bangles clinked softly as she pushed her oversized sunglasses higher on her nose, though the February sky remained stubbornly overcast. The designer shades were more accessory than necessity, but that was the point, wasn't it?

"Champagne, madam?" A staff member appeared at her elbow, offering a tray of crystal flutes. She took one, more for something to do with her hands than any real desire to drink.

The deck was an ecosystem of influence. Melissa, of course, was at the top—her two million followers making her the undisputed queen of this floating kingdom. Then came the Weber twins, identical in their Valentino dresses, their joint account cornering the luxury travel market. Charlotte Ming, the former model turned wellness guru, held court near the bar with her crypto-millionaire husband, both of them dripping in quiet money and loud opinions.

Harper commanded more attention than anyone except Melissa. She was the new darling of social media, famous for her "authentic" approach to luxury living. Her feed was a masterclass in making wealth look effortless. No staged photos, no obvious product placement, just candid shots of her "real life" that happened to feature hundred-dollar yoga pants and ten-thousand-dollar watches.

She'd built her empire on being the anti-influencer influencer, and brands were falling over themselves to work with her. Every post looked like it could have been taken by a friend, every caption read like a text message, and yet everything—everything—was meticulously crafted to appear completely spontaneous. Nicole could see the Cartier bracelet catching the light as Harper gestured to Charlotte, probably describing it as just something she'd "thrown on."

"Nicole, honey!" Melissa glided across the deck, her kaftan catching the wind. Everything about her was calculated, from the arch of her eyebrows to the angle of her hip as she leaned against the railing. "There you are. We simply must get some sunset shots of you and Jen. Where is your better half?"

"Below." The word stuck in Nicole's throat. "She's settling in."

"Well, go get her! Harper's been asking about her, she wants pictures with the two of you."

Nicole's stomach clenched. She'd seen the way Harper looked at Jen during the welcome lunch. The lingering looks, the smiles, the orchestrated moments of 'accidentally' bumping into her.

"Harper's divine, isn't she?" Melissa's voice held something knowing, something sharp beneath the polished surface. "So... authentic. Rather like Jen, wouldn't you say? Though I must admit, I'm surprised you let Jen wear those clothes to lunch."

The criticism stung. Nicole had tried to get Jen to wear the designer outfits she'd selected, but Jen had refused, sticking to her own jeans and white shirt which admittedly, looked great on her.

Before Nicole could defend Jen, movement caught her eye. Jen had emerged on the lower deck, and sure enough, Harper was already making her way toward her. Nicole watched the interaction unfold like a slow-motion car crash.

She couldn't remember the last time she'd felt jealous. She and Jen had always been solid, unshakeable. But watching Harper lean in close to Jen, watching her girlfriend's face soften at whatever Harper was saying—it stung. Nicole clenched her jaw, her nails digging into her palms.

Things had been rocky lately, she couldn't deny that. Their life had started crumbling, revealing cracks in what she'd thought was unshakeable. Jen's words from that night in their kitchen echoed in her mind: *I thought about leaving. Been thinking about it a lot lately.* Maybe Jen wasn't as invested anymore, wasn't as certain about their future as she used to be.

Harper touched Jen's arm, fingers lingering longer than necessary. Leaned in close, whispered something that made Jen laugh for the first time since they'd boarded. Nicole stared, unable to stop herself from watching.

"You might want to get down there," Melissa said. "Before the story becomes something other than what you've planned. Though..." She paused, sipping her champagne. "Maybe that wouldn't be the worst thing. Drama does tend to boost engagement."

Nicole was already moving, phone in hand, snapping a picture of them. As she reached the stairs, she heard that laugh again. The kind of laugh that used to be hers alone.

A cold feeling settled in her chest. She looked down at her camera, at the last shot she'd captured: Jen smiling at Harper, the ocean stretching endless behind them, the sun creating a halo effect. It was the kind of shot that would perform brilliantly on Instagram, but one she knew she would struggle to look at.

Chapter Fourteen

The evening light bathed the *Pacific Dream*'s deck in gold, but Nicole couldn't focus on her shoot. Not when Harper kept appearing, her presence a constant disruption.

"Turn slightly to your left," the photographer directed. "Jen, can you move closer to Nicole?"

Jen slipped an arm around Nicole's waist, pulling her close. For a moment, Nicole forgot about the camera, about Harper, about everything except how much she'd missed this. When was the last time Jen had held her like this? The casual intimacy of it made her throat tight. She leaned into the touch, trying to memorize how it felt—the solid warmth of Jen's body, the reassuring pressure.

"Perfect," the photographer called. "Now look at each other."

Nicole turned, meeting Jen's eyes, and caught a glimpse of the old Jen there—the one who used to look at her like she was the only person in the world. Then came the click of the camera, and just like that, Jen's expression shifted, the authenticity replaced by a vacant smile. The transformation was subtle but devastating. It was a shift that probably wouldn't even show up in the photos but felt like a chasm opening between them.

Nicole felt the tension in her girlfriend's muscles, the way she shifted her weight, like she wanted to escape. They'd been at this for nearly an hour, and while Jen was trying her best to hide it, her patience was clearly wearing thin.

"Maybe we could take five?" she suggested, more for Jen's sake than her own. As the photographer stepped away to check his equipment, she turned to Jen. "You okay?"

"Yeah." Jen rolled her shoulders, trying to work out the stiffness. "Just... how many more shots do we need?"

Nicole caught Harper watching them from across the deck, her gaze lingering a beat too long on Jen. "She seems pretty interested in you," she said, aiming for casual but missing by a mile.

"Who, Harper?" Jen's brow furrowed. "We just get along. She's actually quite good fun and interesting. Did you know she's working on a project to transform unused urban spaces in L.A. into community gardens?"

"Really," Nicole said, unable to curb the hint of sarcasm. "How fascinating."

Jen caught her tone and turned to face her fully. "Hey." She took Nicole's hand, squeezing it. "You have nothing to worry about, okay? Harper's just easy to talk to. And honestly, it's nice to have someone here who doesn't think my work is just some cute hobby."

The slight edge in Jen's voice made Nicole wince. She didn't want to be *that* girlfriend—the jealous, controlling one who couldn't handle her partner having friends. Besides, hadn't she dragged Jen on this trip? Forced her into another performance she clearly didn't want?

"You're right," she said. "I'm being silly."

"Ready to continue?" The photographer had returned and was adjusting the setting for a new lens.

Jen's shoulders slumped slightly, but she gamely resumed her pose. Nicole could see the fatigue settling in—in the strain around Jen's eyes, the way her smile seemed disconnected. She was trying so hard to be supportive, to play along, and Nicole felt a wave of guilt.

"Maybe we should wrap this up," she started to say, but before she could finish, Harper's voice carried across the deck.

"Hey, Jen! Want to see the engine room?" Harper's voice carried on the breeze. "Since you mentioned being interested in seeing how the yacht works…"

Jen hesitated, glancing at Nicole. "Would you mind? I know we're in the middle of—"

"No, go ahead," Nicole said, forcing brightness into her voice. "We're probably done here anyway." She waved a hand, as if she wasn't watching her girlfriend slip further away from her.

Jen follow Harper below deck, their heads bent in conversation. The photographer cleared his throat. "Should we wait, or…?"

"No." Nicole's voice came out sharper than intended. "We're done."

She headed for the bar, ordering something stronger than the prop champagne she'd been holding all day. "Whiskey please. Double. Neat."

"Trouble in paradise?" Melissa materialized beside her, resplendent in a white cashmere dress. Her eyes flickered to the drink the bartender set down. "Careful, honey. There's a fine line between carefree and messy on camera."

The comment was delivered like friendly advice, but

Nicole heard the warning beneath the sugar-coated words. Nothing was ever just a joke with Melissa—every comment was calculated, every observation a potential weapon.

"I can hold my liquor, and Jen and I are fine," Nicole said, forcing a smile.

"But they've hit it off rather well, haven't they?" Melissa said. "Harper has that effect on people. Though I'm sure it's nothing to worry about."

But it *was* something to worry about. Nicole could see it in the way Jen's shoulders had relaxed, the way she smiled around Harper.

"Just between us," Melissa continued, her voice dropping to a conspiratorial whisper, "Harper's had her eye on Jen for a while. Something about a woman who works with her hands..." She let the implication hang in the air.

Nicole took a slow sip of her whiskey, studying Melissa over the rim of her glass. The pieces were falling into place: Harper's sudden inclusion on the trip, the seating arrangements at lunch, even the way Melissa kept drawing attention to Jen and Harper's interactions. Melissa thrived on drama, on the subtle manipulations that kept her followers engaged and hungry for more.

"I'm not worried," Nicole said, her voice honeyed with false warmth. "By the way, it really has been the most wonderful day. Your yacht is just stunning, Melissa. You've outdone yourself."

"Oh, Nicole." Melissa's smile widened, catlike. "This is just the beginning. Tomorrow we're heading further south— the water should be a few degrees warmer and better for snorkeling. I've arranged for a professional underwater photographer." She touched Nicole's arm. "You and Jen do swim, don't you?"

"Of course," Nicole said, knowing full well that Jen

hated cold water and hadn't packed a swimsuit. She'd have to figure that out later.

"Excellent. And then tomorrow night..." Melissa clapped her hands together. "We're having a our pre-valentines dinner. The dresses have all been picked out, every outfit has been sponsored. Yours, and Jen 's of course have been delivered to your cabin. The photos will be amazing."

Nicole nodded, maintaining her smile even as her stomach churned. More opportunities for Harper to hover around Jen. She couldn't stop picturing them down there in the engine room. What was so fascinating about machinery anyway? The yacht's sway suddenly felt unsettling.

"And about Valentine's Day," Melissa's voice sliced through her spiraling thoughts, "our last day at sea will be our *pièce de résistance*. We'll finish with group photos before departing—the brands are particularly excited about those." She paused, examining her manicure. "Everyone looking fabulous and in love. It's what the followers want to see, isn't it?"

The implied threat wasn't lost on Nicole. Everyone who was coupled up needed to look in love or face the consequences. She took another sip of whiskey, letting it burn away the words she couldn't say.

Chapter Fifteen

Executives in tailored suits filled the glass-walled meeting room of the downtown high-rise. Small groups clustered around high tables while others were seated or lined up at the breakfast buffet. Garcia's was catering the tech company's quarterly meeting, and the spread was impressive. Ana balanced another tray of mini quiches and fresh fruit, weaving between the long tables draped in white linens.

The buffet stations held fluffy scrambled eggs studded with fresh herbs, crispy bacon, and maple breakfast sausages. A tower of golden pancakes sat beside bowls of fresh berries and pitchers of warm syrup. At the omelet station, one of the line cooks worked three pans at once, folding eggs around mushrooms, spinach, and cheese. The pastry section overflowed with still-warm croissants, blueberry muffins, and Danish pastries drizzled with vanilla glaze. Fresh fruit platters offered arrangements of melons, pineapple, and strawberries, while silver coffee urns steamed at both ends of the spread.

From the catering kitchen, Ana watched Dani work,

calling out instructions and managing the constant flow of food. Even in the middle of breakfast service, with dozens of hungry executives to feed and multiple stations to oversee, Dani made it all look effortless. Where others might stress or rush, she remained unruffled, handling each new request or minor crisis like it was just another Tuesday. Ever since King Ranch, Ana had been mesmerized by her girlfriend's ability to turn chaos into choreography.

"Fresh croissants coming out!" Dani's voice pulled her from her thoughts. "Ana, we need these on the pastry station, *mi amor*."

Ana grabbed the basket of still-warm pastries, but her phone buzzed before she could move. She'd been trying to resist checking all morning, but...

"Don't do it," Dani called, not even looking up from plating bacon. "Get them out."

Last night, curled up on their couch, pizza box balanced between them, Ana had sworn she was done obsessing over Nicole and Jen's posts. Done comparing their lives. But this morning the notification lingered, tempting her.

"Ana." Dani's voice was closer now. She'd left her station to lean through the service window. "Stop daydreaming."

"Sorry," Ana said, grabbing the croissants. "On it."

She weaved through the crowd, refreshing the pastry station and straightening the neat rows of Danishes. Her phone buzzed again and she was dying to look. For the next hour, Ana focused on her work—refilling coffee urns, clearing used plates, bringing out fresh fruit when the platters started looking sparse. But her mind kept drifting to Nicole and Jen. They'd boarded Melissa St. Clair's yacht yesterday, despite that awful fight Ana had witnessed at the ranch. The first photos had appeared last night. The couple posed on deck, champagne glasses in hand, sunset painting the sky behind them. #YachtLife #ValentinesCruise #Couplegoals #Friends #Blessed 🥂 🌅

Finally, during a lull in service, Ana ducked into the restroom and pulled out her phone, eager to see what she'd missed. The latest post had gone up just twenty minutes ago: Nicole and Jen in their cabin, snuggled up in bed under white satin sheets, a wooden tray between them holding cappuccinos in delicate china cups, fresh croissants, and a bowl of berries. "Cozy morning with my love in our cabin aboard the *Pacific Dream* Thank you @MelissaStClair for the most incredible Valentine's getaway #YachtLife #Love #BlessedWithTheBest"

Ana studied the photo, searching for signs of tension, any hint of the strain she'd witnessed at the ranch. But Jen was smiling, her head resting on Nicole's shoulder as she reached for a strawberry. They looked happy. Relaxed. Like maybe they'd worked things out.

She scrolled through more photos from the previous evening. The couple at dinner with a group of beautiful people, all designer clothes and flawless hair and make-up. Everyone laughing at some shared joke, arms draped casually around each other like old friends. "Dinner with the crew! Nothing better than good food and even better company #YachtLife #Friends #Blessed 💕"

Another shot showed them all on deck, fairy lights twinkling overhead, champagne glasses raised in a toast. Jen was wearing jeans and a white shirt, her arm around Nicole's waist, looking at her with such tenderness that Ana's chest ached. Good. *Good for them.*

She'd been worried after witnessing their fight, had felt guilty for eavesdropping on such a private moment. But maybe that's just what relationships were sometimes—working through the hard parts to get back to the good.

A knock on the bathroom door made her jump. "Ana?" Dani's voice. "You okay in there?"

"Yeah!" She quickly flushed the toilet to maintain the pretense. "Just a minute!"

One last photo caught her eye as she was about to put her phone away. Nicole and Jen on the bow of the yacht, recreating that famous *Titanic* scene. But it was the candid shot after that made Ana pause—both of them laughing, Jen nearly falling, Nicole catching her, their faces close, lost in each other. "Sometimes you just have to be a little silly with the one you love #MyHeart #AlwaysAndForever"

"Ana?" Dani knocked again. "Sorry to interrupt your pee but one of the waiters just quit and the station needs restocking."

Ana opened the door, her phone tucked under her arm as she dried her hands, to find Dani leaning against the wall, arms crossed. She was about to tuck her phone back in her pocket, but Dani had already spotted it.

"You were looking at their posts again, weren't you?"

Ana felt her cheeks flush. "They seem happy. Like, really happy. I think they worked things out."

Dani rolled her eyes good-naturedly and gave Ana a kiss on her cheek before they walked back to the kitchen. "Why do you care so much?"

"I don't know... After seeing them at the ranch, seeing them fight like that, I just wanted them to be okay."

"You've got the biggest heart," Dani said, touching her cheek briefly. "But right now, I need that big heart focused on feeding these executives. They're eating like wolves."

"Yes, chef." Ana smiled, grabbing a fresh tray of bacon. These corporate events weren't so bad, she thought as she restocked the buffet. Breakfast and lunch service meant they'd be done by three. Already she was looking forward to later. They'd take leftovers home, arrange everything on a tray and take it to bed. They still had two episodes left of that crime series they'd been watching, the one where they kept pausing to argue about who the killer was. Dani was convinced it was the sister, but Ana had her money on the neighbor.

Her phone buzzed again. She ignored it, focusing instead on arranging a fresh platter of bacon just the way Dani had taught her. Crispy strips laid out in an overlapping pattern, a sprig of parsley for garnish. It didn't matter that it would be demolished in minutes; what mattered was doing it right. As she headed back out to the buffet, she thought about the photos and hoped Nicole and Jen had found their way back to each other.

Chapter Sixteen

Nicole stood at the railing, her stomach churning as she watched the instructor hand out snorkeling equipment. She hadn't told anyone, not even Jen, about how truly terrified of deep water she really was. It had never mattered before. She'd made sure to stay away from such situations, crafting any water-related content around pools and beach shots.

The Coronado Islands rose from the water like ancient guardians, their volcanic rocks dark against the sky. Several pelicans glided past, riding the thermals, while seabirds wheeled and dove around the rocky outcrops.

"All right, everyone!" The instructor's voice carried across the deck. "Now that we've covered the safety briefing, let's get your wetsuits on. The water's a bit chilly this time of year."

Safety check. Right. The one she'd barely paid attention to, too busy dry-heaving from anxiety.

Jen appeared on deck, zipping up her wetsuit over a borrowed swimsuit. "Excited?" she asked. Harper immediately moved beside her.

"Totally," Harper said, even though the question was meant for Nicole. "Want to go in together?"

The instructor gathered them for final instructions. "The current's not strong, but the water's deep here off the Coronados. If you need help, wave your arm above the surface." He pointed to a cluster of rocky outcrops about two hundred yards away, their dark shapes breaking through the waves. "We're going to swim to those small islands—they're perfect for snorkeling. Lots of fish around the rocks." He traced the route with his hand. "We'll swim over as a group. It's only two hundred yards and perfectly safe."

Nicole stared at the distance between the yacht and the rocks. Two hundred yards of Pacific Ocean. It might as well have been two miles. The choppy water stretched endlessly, deep and dark. She watched a wave crash against the nearest rock, sending spray into the air, and her stomach lurched. Too far. It was too far.

She only half-listened to the instructor's final words, focused instead on controlling her breathing, on not letting anyone see how her hands trembled as she adjusted her mask. Her fear, and her worries about Jen and Harper, were getting the better of her.

"Wait, wait!" Melissa's voice rang out across the deck. "We need a group shot before we get wet." She pulled out her phone, its waterproof case glinting in the sun. "Everyone gather 'round!" The group shuffled into position, arranging themselves in a semicircle. Jen moved automatically to Nicole's left side—muscle memory from countless photos together.

"Say adventure!" Melissa called out, and everyone smiled their Instagram smiles. Nicole's cheeks ached with the effort of looking carefree, of pretending she wasn't about to face her biggest fear while her relationship crumbled around her.

"You okay?" Jen asked. She must have seen something in Nicole's face.

"I'm fine." Nicole adjusted her mask again, unnecessarily.

"Here." Jen reached for her, and for a moment Nicole thought she might kiss her... but no. She was just fixing Nicole's mask strap. "You're all set."

"I suppose we should do this together?" Jen asked.

The words stung, but watching Harper hover nearby, clearly waiting for Jen, anger flooded through her. "No, I'm fine. Harper's waiting for you."

It came out sharp, and she saw a hint of hurt flash across Jen's face before she could hide it. *Good.* Let Jen feel a fraction of what she had been feeling.

One by one, the other couples started entering the water. Nicole stared into the depths, her GoPro attached to the end of her selfie stick. She had to do this. Had to prove something. To Jen, to Harper, to their followers. To herself. She hated the ocean.

Blood thundering in her ears, she stepped off the platform. The coldness of the water was shocking despite the wetsuit, pressing against her like a physical weight. For one terrifying moment, she forgot everything she'd been taught. Water flooded her snorkel, burning her throat. The world blurred into a kaleidoscope of blues and shadows as her lungs seized, fighting against the foreign sensation of breathing through the tube.

Panic rose as she thrashed, trying to remember how to clear her snorkel. But everything was confusion and cold and rising terror. A hand gripped her arm. Not Jen's familiar touch, but the instructor's. Through her mask, his gesture was clear: *relax, breathe normally, follow the group.*

Nicole kicked forward, each movement a battle against her instincts. The other snorkelers glided through the alien landscape with ease, their forms ethereal in the filtered sunlight. She followed, movements robotic, every fiber of her being concentrated on the simple act of breathing: in, out. But it wasn't working. The snorkel felt huge in her mouth, foreign and intrusive. The sound of her own breath rasped in her ears, too loud, too fast, but she couldn't slow it down.

Don't think about the

Then someone shouted—the sound distorted by waves, but the word was unmistakable:

"SHARK!"

Nicole pivoted her head frantically until she located the dorsal fin—heading straight for her. Her world exploded into pure terror.

Nicole fought to keep her head above water, gasping and sputtering, salt water burning her nose. Her lungs heaved as she fought to get air past the panic. She'd already lost track of how far she was from the yacht, her sense of direction scrambled by fear.

"SHARK!"

The cry came again, and Nicole's body went rigid. Through her mask, still fogged and dripping, she saw the others pointing. But she couldn't focus on them. Couldn't focus on anything except the dark shape moving through the water. She kicked wildly, not sure which direction meant safety. The world spun, sky and sea whirling together. She tried to scream but only produced a choked gasp. Her body betrayed her, trying to inhale at exactly the wrong moment, and salt water rushed in. Dark spots danced at the edges of her vision. *Was she drowning?* The last thing she saw before consciousness fled was a fin cutting through the water—smaller than she'd imagined, almost delicate.

Not that it mattered now as the darkness took her.

Chapter Seventeen

Through the spray of water, Jen saw Nicole—too far away, thrashing wildly. *Fuck. Is she panicking?* She'd suspected for years that Nicole had a fear of deep water. But she'd let her irritation and exhaustion from the constant posing keep her at Harper's side. She'd just wanted to escape, one moment away from the circus, to enjoy the water. And now Nicole was out there, alone, panicking.

"Just a Thresher," Harper laughed beside her. "Completely harmless—"

Then Nicole went under.

Jen's world narrowed to a single point. She dove, powerful strokes eating up the distance, her muscles burning with the effort. The ocean fought her, waves pushing against her progress, each second stretching into an eternity. *Too slow. She was moving too damn slow.*

Nicole surfaced, gasping, choking, before she went under again.

No. Not like this.

"Nicole!" The name tore from her throat. Others were

starting to realize something was wrong—the instructor changing direction, voices rising in alarm.

Through the churning water, Jen caught glimpses of blonde hair, and she dove. There, a flash of pale skin. Nicole had stopped moving, her body drifting like seaweed in the current, hair forming a halo around her face. The sight sent ice through Jen's veins.

She grabbed Nicole, one arm locking across her chest in a rescue hold. Nicole's body was deadweight, unresponsive. Jen kicked hard, her muscles screaming. Each second that passed was another second Nicole wasn't breathing.

"Help!" The word ripped from her lips as she broke the surface, raw and desperate. "She's not breathing!"

The instructor reached them first, helping to keep Nicole's face above water as they fought their way back to the yacht. This wasn't happening. This couldn't be happening.

Together, they managed to haul Nicole onto the deck. The instructor immediately began CPR, placing his hands over her chest and pushing hard and fast.

"One, two, three, four..." he counted under his breath, reaching thirty before pausing to deliver two rescue breaths. "Come on, Nicole," he muttered, resuming compressions without hesitation.

"Come on, baby," Jen whispered, her voice breaking. "Please. Please come back to me." She heard voices behind her—Melissa organizing people, someone calling for the ship's medic, worried murmurs growing louder. None of it mattered. Only the terrible stillness of Nicole's face, the way her wet hair clung to her cheeks, the absolute wrongness of her silence.

The instructor continued compressions, his face

focused. "How long was she under?" he asked between breaths.

"Ten seconds. Maybe fifteen." It felt like an eternity.

More footsteps—the ship's medic arriving with an emergency kit. Jen watched him check Nicole's pulse.

And then, Nicole convulsed, seawater pouring from her mouth. It was the most beautiful sound Jen had ever heard. Relief flooded through her as Nicole started coughing. The medic turned her onto her side, helping clear her airway.

That's when Jen noticed the phones coming out. As soon as it was clear Nicole would live, the performance began again. She saw Melissa step forward, probably already crafting the narrative in her head, while others positioned themselves for better angles.

"Give her space!" Jen's voice cracked across the deck. "Back up and put those phones away! What's wrong with you people?" She'd just dragged Nicole's body from the ocean, had watched her fight for breath, had felt the terrifying stillness of her in the water—and they were treating it like content. Like entertainment. A cold rage settled in her as she watched them filming. These people had shared meals with them, had lounged on deck trading stories and drinks, had called themselves friends.

But now, with Nicole's coughed-up seawater still staining the deck, they saw only an opportunity. A story to tell. Something to share. The casual cruelty of it staggered her, but she couldn't find the words, couldn't do anything except try to shield Nicole with her own body.

"That was amazing," Harper's voice cut through the chaos. She dropped to her knees beside Jen, too close, her hand landing on Jen's shoulder. "You're a real hero."

Before Jen could process what was happening, Harper pressed her lips to her cheek. The touch felt wrong, invasive, but Jen's focus remained on Nicole, watching for any sign of consciousness returning.

Nicole coughed again, the sound sending waves of relief through Jen's body. Then slowly, Nicole's eyes fluttered open. For a split second, Jen saw only confusion in those familiar blue eyes—then awareness dawned. Nicole's gaze shifted from Jen's face to Harper's lips, still hovering near Jen's cheek, and Jen watched as understanding washed across Nicole's features.

"Baby, you're back," she choked out, tears spilling down her cheeks. She reached for Nicole's hand. "God, I thought I'd lost you. I thought—"

But Nicole's eyes had gone distant, vacant. She turned her face away from both of them, salt water still trailing from her lips. The medic was saying something about shock, about getting her below deck, but Nicole's withdrawal felt like more than physical trauma. Where moments ago Jen had been terrified of Nicole's stillness, now her girlfriend's consciousness felt equally devastating. Nicole was awake, alive, and deliberately turning away from her.

"Nic, please," Jen whispered, her voice cracking. "Look at me."

But Nicole kept her gaze fixed on some point in the distance, her jaw clenched tight. Even as the medic helped her sit up, even as Jen tried to support her other side, Nicole remained rigid, unreachable. The only acknowledgment she gave was to pull her hand from Jen's grasp, the movement subtle but devastating in its finality.

The moment stretched between them like a physical thing. Nicole, pale and shivering but determinedly distant. Jen, reaching for someone who was right there but somehow already gone. And Harper, finally sensing the weight of what she'd done, backing away with a murmured apology that came too late to matter.

Nicole had nearly died, and instead of finding comfort in Jen's arms when she returned to consciousness, she'd found betrayal. The fact that it wasn't what it looked like didn't matter. Not when everything between them lately had been balanced on such a precarious edge already.

The medic helped Nicole to her feet. She swayed slightly but caught herself, refusing Jen's steadying hand. Without a word, she allowed herself to be led below deck while Jen hovered behind, aching to help but knowing her touch wasn't welcome.

"She'll need to keep warm," the medic said, turning to look at Jen as they reached their cabin. "Turn the heating up. She needs to rest. Don't lock the door; I'll come and check on her every hour until she's back to normal."

"Thank you. I'll take it from here," Jen said. "I'll get her in a warm shower and help her into bed—"

"No." Nicole's voice was rough. "I'd rather be alone."

"Nic—"

"Please." She wouldn't meet Jen's eyes, her gaze fixed on the cabin door. "I just... I need to be alone right now."

Chapter Eighteen

Nicole paced the yacht's cabin, each breath feeling tighter than the last. The walls pressed in around her, the small space growing smaller with every passing minute. Three steps this way, four steps that way—no matter how she moved, she couldn't escape the suffocating sensation.

Hours had passed since the medical checks, but the memory of water closing over her head, of pressure building in her chest, refused to fade. Each time the yacht rolled with the waves, her stomach churned, a bitter taste rising in her throat.

She pressed her forehead against the cool glass of the porthole, watching the waves slap against the hull just inches away. All that ocean, right there, separated by mere inches of steel—the vast, indifferent sea that had nearly pulled her under, waiting just on the other side.

Nicole closed her eyes, trying to slow her breathing. She needed air, real air, not the recycled atmosphere pumping through the yacht's vents. But there was nowhere to go, no escape from the tightness in her chest, the panic that clawed at her edges.

She sank down onto the edge of the bed, hands trembling. The walls seemed to inch closer, the ceiling lower. She needed to get out, to breathe. Focusing on the yacht's sounds, she latched onto the faint hum of activity from the kitchen, where staff prepared for the Valentine's Eve dinner. She moved toward it, drawn by the promise of distraction.

Through the service door, she could hear the kitchen humming with activity. Better to focus on that than the memory of water filling her lungs, of consciousness slipping away, of surfacing to see—

No. Don't think about that. Don't think about Jen's face with Harper's lips pressed to her cheek. Don't think about how everything she thought she knew had washed away in that endless ocean.

"Nicole!" Melissa's voice cut through her thoughts. "There you are, darling. We missed you at lunch."

Nicole forced a smile, though her chest tightened at the thought of facing everyone. "Just needed some rest."

"Of course, of course." Melissa's sympathy felt practiced, disingenuous. "But you should join us for dinner. It's our pre-Valentine's celebration, after all." She touched Nicole's arm. "Everyone's been so worried. Especially Harper—she feels terrible about the whole misunderstanding."

That "misunderstanding" hung between them, an invisible and unwelcome presence. Nicole wanted to laugh, or maybe scream. Instead, she nodded, the influencer inside her taking over. "Of course. I'll be there."

"Great." Melissa's smile widened. "And don't worry about Jen. These things happen on trips like this. Sometimes we discover things about ourselves, about our relationships..." She let the implication linger. "The brands love a good drama, you know. Your engagement will skyrocket."

Nicole felt furious. Even this—her near-death experience, her heartbreak—was just content to Melissa. Just another story to sell.

"I should get ready," she said, stepping back.

"That Zimmermann dress is going to be perfect on you," Melissa gushed. "The color, the cut—you'll be the star of the show."

In their cabin, Nicole found the dress that had been delivered earlier—a stunning Zimmermann creation in champagne silk charmeuse. The fabric shimmered under the lights, its soft drape promising to hug her curves. *Turning heads and making statements—her life's sole purpose.*

It lay across the bed like a ghost. Jen's things were still there, scattered across her side of the cabin—her practical clothes a stark contrast to the glamour surrounding them. But Jen herself hadn't returned, not since she'd sent her away.

Nicole's fingers trembled as she reached for her phone. No messages from Jen. But there were hundreds of notifications—comments, DMs, all asking about the incident. Someone had filmed it, of course. Her near-drowning, Jen's rescue, Harper's kiss—all of it already online, already being dissected by strangers.

"Living for this drama!" one comment read. "Team Harper or Team Nicole?"

She put the phone down, feeling sick. *When had their life become this? When had their love story become content for others to consume?*

A knock at the cabin door startled her from her thoughts, and her heart stopped. *Jen? Could it be?*

"Ms. Rivers?" The steward's voice rose, questioning if Nicole was indeed in her cabin.

Grudgingly, Nicole opened the door and was faced with a bunch of red and white roses. *Another prop.*

"Ms. St. Clair's compliments," he said, placing the arrangement on the already crowded vanity.

Nicole stared at her reflection in the mirror, at the woman she barely recognized anymore. The dress waited on the bed, a transformation into someone else's fantasy. She thought of Jen's face this morning, of the genuine fear in her eyes at the thought of losing her. That had been real. That had mattered.

"Ms. Rivers?" The steward hesitated at the door. "Ms. St. Clair asked me to remind you that photos begin at 7:00 p.m."

Nicole nodded, not trusting her voice. As the door closed behind him, she reached for the dress. Her hands brushed against the fabric, soft and expensive and utterly wrong—like everything else she'd created in their life.

Through the porthole, she saw the sun was beginning to set, painting the ocean in shades of gold and pink. Somewhere on this boat, Jen was probably helping the crew with something practical, finding comfort in real work while Nicole hid in their cabin playing dress-up.

She thought of their house in Calabasas, of the mortgage payments that kept her awake at night, of the performances that had become their life, of Jen's face when she'd turned away this morning, hurt and guilty and tired.

Her phone buzzed again. Another message from Melissa: "Hair and makeup will be there in twenty, honey. Unless you're going for the 'authentic, just-survived-a-near-drowning' look? Either way, let's make sure you're camera-ready. We have a narrative to maintain!"

Nicole picked up the dress. For a moment, she could see it all so clearly—the photos they'd take, the story they'd tell: the perfect Valentine's Eve celebration aboard a luxury yacht. #blessed #couplegoals #luxury

Then she thought of the cold water, of the moment she'd blacked out, of how none of their followers or likes or curated photos had mattered then. Only Jen had mattered.

She hung the dress back in the closet and sat on the bed, waiting. Jen would have to come back, eventually, and when she did, Nicole would have to decide—continue the performance or finally let themselves be real.

Outside, the yacht's horn sounded, announcing the approach of evening. Time for another show to begin.

Chapter Nineteen

Darkness settle over the Pacific while Nicole remained in her robe, the untouched Zimmermann dress hanging in the closet. Her phone buzzed with irritated messages from Melissa about missing the sunset photoshoot. The yacht's sway was a little nauseating. It felt like a reminder of how everything in her life was off-balance.

A soft knock broke the silence—not the medic's businesslike rap or Melissa's impatient tapping, but a hesitant, almost broken sound.

"Nic?" Jen's voice, barely audible. "Please. Can I come in?"

Nicole stared at the door, her heart hammering. The memory of water filling her lungs warred with the image of Harper's lips against Jen's cheek.

"It's open," she managed.

The door creaked open slowly. Jen stood in the threshold, still in her jeans and sweater, her face raw with emotion. Her eyes were red-rimmed, her hair disheveled from the ocean and hours of running her hands through it—

a nervous habit Nicole knew well. She looked exhausted, destroyed.

Jen stepped inside, closing the door behind her. Everything unsaid between them filled the small cabin. She took another step forward, then stopped, as if afraid to come closer.

"You're not dressed," Jen said finally, glancing at the untouched gown. "Melissa's looking for you."

"I'm not going."

"You stopped breathing today." Jen's voice cracked. "In my arms, you just... stopped. And now you won't even look at me."

"I saw enough," the words came out sharp, brittle.

"That's not fair." Jen's voice rose slightly. "You know that's not what happened. Harper—"

"Don't." Nicole spun around. "Don't say her name."

They stood facing each other, the yacht's rocking making their subtle swaying seem like a broken dance. Above them, footsteps crossed the deck. The party was beginning without them, life moving on while they remained frozen in this moment.

"I thought I'd lost you," Jen whispered. "When I pulled you out, when you weren't breathing..." She drew a shaky breath, her hands trembling at her sides. "And then you came back, and you looked at me like I was a stranger."

"You let her kiss you."

"I didn't let her... She just did it, and it was on the cheek! After I'd just saved your life!" Jen ran a hand through her hair again, frustrated. "The only thing I was focused on was you. But you're focusing on that, on her? Not the fact that you almost drowned?"

"Does it matter? Does anything matter? Everything's content for them now!" Nicole nodded up toward the main deck where the muffled voices of guests gathered. Her voice broke. "Even my drowning. Everyone had their phones out. Click, click, click." She mimicked taking photos. "Perfect dramatic content."

"I yelled at them to put their phones away. I tried to shield you," Jen said, stepping closer.

"While Harper's lips were on your cheek?"

"Stop it." Jen's voice hardened. "Just stop. You want to talk about betrayal? How about you deleting my gardening appointments so you could drag me to your own events? How about you turning our entire relationship into content?"

Nicole sank onto the bed and buried her face in her hands. "I'm so tired, Jen."

"Of what?"

"Of pretending. Of watching you pull away from me a little more each day." She looked up at Jen—really looked at her—for the first time since the incident. "Of being terrified that if we stop pretending, there isn't anything left."

Jen's face softened. She sat beside Nicole, close but not touching.

"You want to know why I've been spending time with Harper?"

Nicole's chest tightened, but she nodded.

"Because she asked me about my work. My real work. Not as your prop, or the diversity quota, but as a landscaper. She actually listened when I talked about things I'm passionate about." Jen's voice wavered. "When was the last time you asked me about my job, Nic? About my dreams? When was the last time we had a conversation that wasn't about content?"

The question stopped Nicole cold. She couldn't remember.

"I miss you," Jen continued. "The real you. The one who used to get, like, so excited about light and shadow, who'd wake me up at dawn because the morning fog was doing something beautiful. Now everything's just..."

"Content," Nicole finished. She reached for Jen's hand, relief flooding through her when Jen didn't pull away. "I miss that me too, as much as I miss you. I miss us."

From the deck above, they could hear music starting. The Valentine's Eve dinner was beginning without them. Somewhere, close by, Melissa was likely furious.

"I don't want to go back up there," Nicole whispered. "I don't want to, like, pose or play my part."

"Then don't." Jen squeezed her hand. "Let's stay here. We don't owe them anything."

"The house—"

"We'll sell it. Like we talked about. Start over."

Nicole turned to face Jen fully. "What if we left at the next port? Find a hotel and take it from there."

"You mean skip Melissa's big Valentine's Day shoot?" A smile tugged at Jen's lips. "She'd be so pissed."

"Good."

Jen studied her for a long moment. "You're serious."

"Nearly dying has a way of clarifying things." Nicole managed a weak smile. "I choose you. If you'll still have me."

Instead of answering, Jen leaned forward and kissed her. Not for the cameras, not for their followers, but for them. It was soft at first, tentative, searching, like they were learning each other again. Then Nicole's hands found Jen's face, pulling her closer, and the kiss deepened. Jen tasted like home, and when Jen's fingers tangled in her hair, something inside Nicole broke, then mended itself. This was them, real and raw, finding their way back to each other while the world spun on without them.

When they finally parted, breathless, Jen traced Nicole's cheek with trembling fingers. "I love you," she whispered.

Relief washed over Nicole at the words, at the honesty in Jen's voice. She hadn't heard her say that in so long, and she didn't know how much she'd needed it until now. "I love you too," she said. For the first time in years, the words were simply true and belonged only to them.

Chapter Twenty

"Nicole?" Melissa's voice carried through the cabin door, followed by sharp knocks. "Darling, everyone's waiting. I need that Zimmermann dress in the shot. They're paying to have it front and center in this evening's shoot, and you've already missed the sunset."

Nicole tensed on the bed, her eyes drifting to the dress hanging in the closet. The price tag alone could have covered their mortgage payment.

"She's not feeling well enough for dinner," Jen said as she opened the door a crack, using her body to create a barrier.

"Don't be ridiculous." Melissa's voice hardened. "She nearly drowned, and everyone is waiting for her comeback. And yours," she added. "This timing couldn't be more perfect." She tried to peer around Jen. "Nicole, at least let the makeup artist—"

"Melissa, she needs rest - we're not coming to dinner." Jen passed the dress through the gap before closing the door firmly and leaning against it.

Silence stretched for several seconds before Melissa spoke again, her voice tight with anger. "There will be consequences. You can't just pick and choose what you want to do..."

Nicole sat, her knees drawn up to her chest. She chanced a nervous glance at Jen, who grimaced and then gave a shrug. The cabin fell silent after Melissa's footsteps faded. Jen stayed at the door for a moment before turning back to Nicole.

"Thank you," Nicole said. "For making her leave."

Jen crossed to the bed and sat next to her. "You don't have to thank me. I should have been protecting you all along. From her, from all of it."

"I was too caught up in my own world. I wouldn't have listened." Nicole reached for her, fingers trembling slightly as they traced Jen's jaw. "But I'm listening now. I've missed you so much."

"I'm right here." Jen smiled and leaned in, her lips brushing against Nicole's.

Nicole welcomed her mouth, her hands moving to Jen's waist, pulling her closer. Jen cupped Nicole's face, her fingers threading through her hair, drawing her head back, and Nicole moaned softly, her body arching against Jen's. They broke apart for a moment, gasping for air.

Nicole's eyes, dark and intense, met Jen's. "Let's forget about the dress," she whispered. "Let's forget about Melissa. Let's just forget and..." Her gaze lingered on Jen's strong arms and shoulders, her muscular thighs. She longed for her.

Jen's eyes darkened. "You want to..."

Nicole nodded, a mischievous glint in her eyes. "I want to. It's been too long."

Jen grinned and reached for the belt of Nicole's robe.

She tugged, causing the robe to fall open, revealing Nicole's curves beneath. She bit down on her lip, her eyes taking in the sight as her hands slid beneath the silk, tracing Nicole's hip, her fingers lingering on soft skin.

Nicole shivered, a low moan escaping her. She had Jen back, truly back. The certainty of it washed over her like a wave of peace. For the first time in so long, she felt wanted, and she knew that everything would be okay. Whatever path their life took next didn't matter, as long as they put each other first.

Jen nudged her back on the bed and leaned over her, her lips trailing a path down Nicole's neck, leaving goosebumps in their wake. Her mouth found Nicole's breast, her tongue swirling around the sensitive peak, making Nicole gasp.

"Fuck, Jen..." Nicole arched into her touch, her hands reaching for the hem of Jen's sweatshirt, pulling it up and over her head.

Jen had already unfastened her jeans. She slid them down and kicked them off, leaving her only in a sports bra and briefs. A slow, appreciative smile grew as she took in the sight of Nicole. "You're beautiful," she murmured. "So beautiful."

Nicole smiled, her heart swelling with a love she thought she'd lost. "So are you. Come here." She pulled Jen down, their mouths colliding in a hungry, desperate kiss. Her hands tangled in Jen's hair, pulling her down on top of her. The weight of Jen settling on her body was both exhilarating and grounding. She was finally whole again. Jen's skin, warm and smooth, pressed against hers, a perfect fit.

Jen's heart beat fast against Nicole's, mirroring her racing pulse as they kissed and moved together. Jen's hands, strong and sure, explored Nicole's body.

"Let me show you how much I've missed you," Jen whispered, moving lower, her lips trailing the valley between Nicole's breasts. Her hands slid down Nicole's sides, tracing her hips and her thighs. Nicole grabbed Jen's shoulders, her nails digging into her skin as Jen kissed her ribs and her stomach, the touch of her lips featherlight and teasing. A low moan escaped her lips as she bucked her hips. She couldn't take it any more. This slow, deliberate torment was driving her wild.

Jen's mouth found the sensitive skin above Nicole's pubic bone. She kissed her gently, then more deeply, her tongue moving down to trace her folds, eliciting a series of low moans from Nicole.

Her tongue brushed against Nicole's clit, teasing it with gentle flicks. Nicole trembled, bucked, her breathing ragged. Jen, sensing her need, upped the pressure, circling her tongue, exploring her, each touch intensifying and building the pleasure within her. Her hands clamped onto Nicole's hips.

"Yes!" Nicole cried out. "Please don't stop." Nicole's body writhed beneath Jen, her hands fisting the sheets, then shifting to her hair and her shoulders, her breath coming in quick gasps. Jen changed her position, her tongue now a rhythmic drumbeat as Nicole's vision blurred, the world contracting and expanding in sensation.

Then, it hit her – a wave of pure, unadulterated bliss, washing over her, leaving her breathless and spent. Jen pulled back, her eyes searching Nicole's face.

Nicole's chest was heaving, her eyes glazed over, a blissful smile playing on her lips. "Was that...?" Jen faltered, her eyes hopeful.

Nicole nodded, still catching her breath. "That was

amazing." She reached up and ran her fingers through Jen's hair. "I haven't felt like that in... I don't even know."

Jen smiled and moved up to kiss her. The day's worries faded away in the heat of their embrace, and for a moment, Nicole was lost in a feeling of perfect contentment. Jen was the familiar comfort of home, a sense of belonging that had been achingly absent from her life lately.

With a playful grin, Nicole reversed their positions, straddling Jen's hips, settling her weight on top of her. "My turn," she whispered with a flirtatious smile. She leaned in, brushing her lips against Jen's collarbone. "Do you remember that time in our old apartment, when we broke the bed frame?"

Jen laughed and rolled her eyes good-naturedly. "Yes, I believe that was your doing." Her fingers traced lazy patterns over Nicole's hips, making her shiver. "Three months' of savings gone in one very energetic night."

"Worth it, though." Nicole chuckled. "I bet I can do that again.

Chapter Twenty-One

Dawn was breaking over the Pacific as Nicole and Jen made their way to the stern. The yacht had anchored just outside Ensenada's harbor during the night—close enough to see the port city's lights twinkling along the coastline. The tender bobbed against the yacht's hull, where one of the crew, already waiting, reached up to take their bags.

Nicole adjusted her borrowed USC hoodie, the fabric soft and worn against her skin. After years of agonizing over every outfit, the simple jeans and sweatshirt felt like freedom.

"Going somewhere?" Melissa's voice cut through the morning quiet. She stood on the upper deck in a silk robe, coffee cup in hand. "The Valentine's Day briefing starts in an hour. Make sure you're back in time."

Nicole tightened her grip on the railing as she prepared to climb down into the waiting tender. "We're leaving."

"Don't be ridiculous." Melissa's voice hardened. "The brands are expecting content. Your contracts—"

"Are void," Jen cut in, steadying Nicole as she made the

descent. "Check the fine print. Near-death experiences tend to nullify influencer agreements."

Melissa's laugh echoed across the water. "Near-death? Please. It was barely a dip in the ocean. Though I must say, the footage performed brilliantly." She leaned over the railing, looking down at them. "Think about what you're doing, Nicole. Walking away from this... you'll be toxic. No brand will touch you. Your career will be over."

"My career?" Nicole's voice shook slightly. "I almost died yesterday. I stopped breathing. And all you care about is content?"

"Of course I care about content." Melissa's smile was cold. "It's what we do. It's who we are."

"No." Nicole settled into the tender, Jen's arm steady around her waist. "It's who *you* are. I'm done."

"You'll be nothing without this." Melissa gestured around the yacht. "Without me. Another month and you'll be irrelevant."

"Better irrelevant than losing what's important." Nicole squeezed Jen's hand. "Jen's more important than any of this." She motioned to the yacht, the whole charade that seemed to sum up Melissa. "I choose us. It's really that simple."

"How sweet." Melissa's voice dripped with sarcasm. "And how will you pay that mortgage in Calabasas? How will you maintain that lifestyle your followers expect?"

"As I said, I'm done." Nicole looked up at Melissa. "Whatever we do next is no one's business." The morning light was harsh and unforgiving. Where she'd once seen glamour and success, she now saw only exhaustion. Dark circles. Fine lines deepened. Eyes sharp with a hunger that could never be satisfied. Without the lighting, without the careful angles and filtered photos, without the designer clothes and professionally styled hair, Melissa St. Clair was just... human. She always had been. Just a woman with good marketing skills, nothing more. Nicole felt a strange mix of pity and embarrassment—pity for the desperate woman above them, forever chasing the next sponsorship, the next wave of validation, and embarrassment that she'd ever placed her on such a pedestal. She'd spent years trying to become this woman, trying to emulate something that was an illusion, a constructed image for the cameras and the followers.

"You'll regret this," Melissa called, as the crew member started the tender's engine. "When you're working regular jobs like regular people, you'll miss being special."

Nicole shook her head. "That's the thing, Melissa. I was never special. I just had good lighting."

The tender pulled away, its motor humming as it cut through the morning swells. Nicole watched the Pacific Dream grow smaller, Melissa's figure becoming a tiny dot against the sky. Other faces appeared at the rails—the Weber twins, Charlotte Ming, Harper—all watching their departure like audience members at a play.

The marina lay ahead, pleasure boats and fishing vessels coming to life as the day began. Nicole leaned into Jen, resting her head on her shoulder, breathing in her scent. She closed her eyes and smiled, letting the gentle motion of the boat and the steady presence of Jen's arm around her wash away her old life. They had no plan, no idea what came next, but for the first time in years, that felt like freedom rather than failure.

"Are you okay?" Jen asked.

"Yeah. I'm okay." Nicole kissed her and rested her forehead against Jen's. "I need to write one last post. Do you mind?"

Jen studied her face, a mix of hope and uncertainty in her eyes. "The last?"

"Yes. The very last."

"Go ahead, babe." Jen smiled. "I never thought I'd hear those words."

Nicole pulled out her phone, opened Instagram, and after a moment's hesitation, began to type:

"For years, I've shared every moment of my life with you. My morning routine that left me no time to even drink my coffee, my meticulously plated meals that went cold while I photographed them, my adventures that were more about the post than the experience, my relationship reduced to poses and hashtags, even our home staged like a movie set. But yesterday, I nearly drowned - not just in the ocean, but in the pressure to be someone I'm not. Today, I choose reality. Love over likes. Truth over trending. This will be my last post. Thank you for being part of my journey, but it's time for me to live my life instead of performing it. - Nicole"

She hit post, then, before she could second-guess herself, turned off her phone. For the first time in years, she let the screen go dark. Had she ever turned it off before? She couldn't remember. It felt strange, but good—like taking off shoes that had been too tight. Now, she could wear clothes that felt comfortable instead of just looking good. Maybe she'd go back to marketing, get a job with regular hours where she could actually leave work at work. They could spend evenings together on the couch, sharing takeout and watching bad TV. They could travel somewhere without having to document every moment, could have lazy Sundays where they never changed out of their pajamas, could have friends over for dinner without staging the table, could cook together in the kitchen without worrying about the lighting.

"What are you thinking about?" Jen asked, watching her face.

"I want breakfast," she said, surprising herself with how simple and true the words felt. "Real breakfast. Something messy and delicious, like pancakes dripping with syrup and bacon on the side." She could order what she wanted now, eat what she craved rather than what photographed well. The day stretched ahead of them, wide open with possibility. No schedules, no shoots, no posts.

"I'm with you, babe. Let's find the greasiest breakfast place in Ensenada. Just you and me and good food and strong coffee." She kissed Nicole's temple. "I want to sit across from you and talk about nothing and everything."

Nicole smiled. "I'd like that. I can't remember the last time we just... had breakfast together."

"I know," Jen said, pulling her closer. "But we have all the time in the world now."

Chapter Twenty-Two

Ana slumped against their apartment door, exhausted from her night shift and a little bewildered. She'd been constantly checking her phone after seeing Nicole's final post. A few hours later, her account had vanished. "Can you believe they just... left?" she called out, dropping her bag. "Like, completely deleted everything?"

"Baby, I know you followed them for a long time, but it sounds like they needed a change. Good for them." Dani's back was toward her, still in her sleep shorts and tank top, cooking. "Come eat something."

The smell of coffee and something sweet drew Ana in. Pancakes. Not just regular pancakes—heart-shaped ones, golden brown and perfectly fluffy. Her stomach growled in anticipation. "You know me too well."

"Come on, how could I not make your favorite?" Dani grinned over her shoulder. "It's Valentine's Day, and my girl just worked a twelve-hour shift."

"Mmm, I love you." Ana wrapped her arms around Dani's waist from behind. "It's just weird, you know," she continued. "It's like a part of my daily routine is just... gone. All those posts, all those memories—gone. Just... poof."

"Isn't that kind of the point?" Dani flipped a pancake. "They're choosing real memories over posts."

"I know, but..." Ana rested her chin on Dani's shoulder. "I followed them for so long. Even after seeing them at the ranch, seeing how complicated it was... I still checked their posts every day. It felt like I knew them."

"But you didn't," Dani said. "You knew what they wanted you to see."

"Yeah." Ana sighed. "I hope they're okay though. That last post... it felt real. Like *really* real."

Dani turned in Ana's arms, studying her face. "You're upset."

"Not upset exactly. Just..." Ana searched for the words. "It's like when you finish a really good romance novel. You're happy for the characters, but you also miss them already."

"Well..." Dani slid the last pancake onto a plate and placed it on the small table. "Speaking of romance... I may have swapped my evening shift."

Ana's eyes widened as she sat. "But you never get Valentine's night off."

"I guess I just got lucky." Dani winked. "And you need to find something nice to wear for later. I have a surprise."

"Baby..." Ana's heart swelled with warmth and a twinge of guilt. She'd been so caught up in her night shifts and following Nicole's drama that she hadn't even thought about Valentine's Day plans. She'd just assumed it would be like any other day—she would sleep while Dani worked. But here was Dani, making heart-shaped pancakes and planning surprises, and she hadn't done a thing. She gave Dani a hopeful look. "So, where are we going?"

"I told you, it's a surprise." Dani's eyes twinkled. "And before you start begging—no, I'm seriously not telling you."

Ana took a bite of the pancakes as she studied her girlfriend's face, trying to read her expression. The pancakes were delicious, and she moaned, closing her eyes as she ate. "You're being sneaky," she mumbled through a mouthful.

"Yep." Dani gave her a kiss on her cheek before heading to the bathroom. "Now eat and sleep," she called over her shoulder. "You've been up all night."

* * *

Hours later, Ana emerged, feeling refreshed and relaxed, to find Dani dressed in her best chinos and a freshly ironed button-down shirt. The sight made her breath catch—Dani could pull off fancy just as well as she did chef's blacks and softball uniforms.

"You clean up nice, chef," she said, taking in how the shirt stretched across Dani's shoulders.

"You don't look so bad yourself," Dani said softly, her eyes lingering on Ana's simple black dress. She stepped closer, running her fingers along Ana's bare arm. "Almost makes me want to cancel our plans and stay right here."

"Oh yeah?"

"Mmhmm." Dani pulled her closer, then glanced at her phone. "But our ride's waiting, and we'll have plenty of time in bed later."

They made their way down the stairs, Dani's hand on the small of Ana's back. At the landing, she gave Ana's behind a playful smack, making her yelp and giggle. It felt like their first date all over again—the butterflies, the anticipation. Dani had always been good at surprises, even back then.

They held hands in the Uber, fingers intertwined, a comfortable silence between them, punctuated by small, excited glances. The car pulled over at their favorite taco truck, and Ana watched as Dani picked up two bags of takeout that were already waiting.

"This can't be the whole surprise," Ana said. "You're too dressed up for just tacos."

"Patience." Dani grinned as they turned a corner. "Are you ready?"

The Uber dropped them outside a modest house in Virginia Heights. Ana's brow furrowed as she recognized it immediately as Dani's uncle's place.

"Tío Miguel's?" she asked, her confusion deepening. "What are we doing here? Are we spending Valentine's with your uncle?"

Dani threw her head back and laughed, then shook her head. "No, baby. I'd never do that to you." She got out of the car and opened the door for Ana, offering her hand.

The neighborhood was alive with its usual sounds—kids playing basketball down the street, *música norteña* drifting from somewhere nearby, the occasional car rumbling past with its bass thumping - the familiar soundtrack of their life together.

A chain-link fence surrounded Tío Miguel's yard, and the concrete driveway was cracked but swept clean. As Ana's eyes adjusted to the twilight, her gaze fell on something she hadn't noticed before, and her breath caught in her throat. There, nestled beside the garage, was a boat. Not a yacht, not anything fancy, but a small sailboat, its hull a faded blue, its mast reaching toward the darkening sky. The small vessel was adorned with strings of twinkling fairy lights, which seemed wonderfully out of place in the working-class neighborhood. The lights reflected off the hull, creating a glow that transformed the ordinary driveway into something special.

"What's this?" she asked, looking up in surprise and wonder.

"This," Dani said, gesturing toward the boat with a flourish, "is our Valentine's Day adventure." She stepped closer, her voice dropping to a soft, intimate murmur. "It's not a luxury yacht, but I'd sail anywhere in the world with you if I could."

Ana's heart melted. She looked from the boat to Dani's face, her eyes shining with love. A small table was set up on the deck, complete with a checkered tablecloth, two glasses, and a flickering candle. A bucket of ice held four bottles of Corona.

"Oh, Dani," Ana breathed, kissing Dani's hand. "It's beautiful."

"Well…" Dani helped her onto the deck. "I figured if they can have their Pacific Dream, we can have ours. Even if it's on blocks in my uncle's driveway."

Ana laughed as she settled onto the cushioned seat, watching Dani pour their beers into actual glasses—a touch of class that made her smile.

"I know it isn't fancy," Dani said softly, "and we're not drinking champagne, but when I'm with you, I always feel like a *millonaria*. I don't need all that other stuff."

Ana leaned in over the table, capturing Dani's lips in a slow, tender kiss. "It's perfect," she whispered. "You're perfect." She took Dani's hand, her heart full, and together they looked up at the stars, the little boat in the driveway feeling like the most magical place in the world.

Chapter Twenty-Three

The tiny Ensenada café, a world away from the luxury of the yacht, was already bustling when Nicole and Jen slipped into a corner booth. The vinyl seats were cracked and worn, the table slightly wobbly, but the air was rich with the aroma of fresh coffee and sizzling chorizo. Outside, waves crashed against the breakwater, and seagulls wheeled past the foggy windows. A radio behind the counter played old *rancheras*, the melancholic vocals mixing with the clatter of plates and murmured conversations in Spanish and English.

"What can I get you?" The waitress appeared, notepad in hand, her lined face kind. She wore a name tag that read 'Rosa' and carried herself with the easy confidence of someone who had been serving breakfast in this café for decades. Nicole and Jen exchanged a grateful smile – they were famished.

Nicole glanced at Jen, then smiled. "Everything," she said. "We're starving." Her stomach growled as if on cue, making Rosa chuckle.

They ordered with abandon—*huevos rancheros* with

extra salsa, crispy *chilaquiles* smothered in *crema*, fresh tortillas, steaming coffee served in thick ceramic mugs. It was a far cry from the meticulously plated meals they'd endured on the yacht. While they waited, Nicole watched the morning crowd: fishermen fresh off their boats, construction workers in paint-splattered clothes, a couple of surfers with salt-crusted hair. The café felt like a refuge, a place outside of time where nobody knew their names or their story.

When the food arrived, they dove in without a thought for presentation or aesthetics, sauce dripping, yolks breaking, pure pleasure in the mess and flavor of it all. The *chilaquiles* were delicious—crisp yet tender, the sauce spicy enough to make Nicole's eyes water. The tortillas came wrapped in a cloth napkin, still steaming.

"God, I forgot what it's like to actually eat while food is hot," Nicole said around a mouthful of *chilaquiles*. She'd rolled up the sleeves of her borrowed hoodie, and there was salsa on her chin. Jen reached across the table to wipe it away.

"So what now?" Jen asked.

Nicole took a long sip of coffee, savoring the bitter warmth. "I was thinking," she said. "Remember that TentBox you bought last year?" Jen's eyebrows shot up in surprise.

"It's still in the box in the garage as you blatantly refused to go camping with me." Her tone was light, but Nicole caught the hint of old hurt beneath the words, and her stomach clenched with guilt.

"I was an idiot," she said with a wince, tracing the rim of her coffee mug. "But how about we finally put it to good use? We could go away for a few days, just the two of us?

Your schedule is open this week and I'm…" She let out a chuckle. "Well, I have all the time in the world."

"Really? You mean it?" Jen's eyes lit up when Nicole nodded, and she reached across the table and caught Nicole's hand. A warmth spread through Nicole's chest at the hopeful expression on Jen's face. "Where to?"

Nicole leaned forward, her free hand gesturing with growing animation. "Well, we could fly home today, pack a bag, and maybe drive out to Joshua Tree? Remember how we always talked about going there, getting away from the city? We could watch the sunset, count the stars…" The words tumbled out faster now, as if she couldn't contain them.

A wicked smile spread across Jen's face. "S'mores?"

"Yeah. Real ones, over a campfire. Not the deconstructed artisanal ones Melissa serves." They both laughed at that, the sound drawing a curious glance from Rosa as she refilled their coffee cups. "Just us, under the stars, being completely insignificant."

"And we'll put the house on the market as soon as we get back," Nicole continued. "I'll even sell my car. But right now? Right now, we need this. Time to just… be us again." Jen's hand tightened around hers, her eyes shining with unshed tears.

"Okay, let's do it. You, me and the desert." Jen paused for a second. "And I love you, babe. I love the you that's sitting here with messy hair and borrowed clothes, planning our escape over runny eggs and bottom-of-the-pot coffee."

Nicole felt tears prick at her eyes. "I love you too," she whispered. "Hopefully this'll be the first camping trip of many. I know we won't be able to afford Hawaii anytime soon, and honestly? That's okay with me." She shook her head, letting out a quiet breath. "God, what was I so afraid of? That everything would fall apart if I stopped being an influencer? That I'd become... insignificant?" She gave a short laugh, the sound carrying equal parts disbelief and relief. "It all seems so ridiculous now. The only thing that matters—the only thing that's ever really mattered—is you. This. Us. Love. That's it. That's everything."

Jen held up her coffee mug in a mock toast. "That's it, babe. Love." She paused, a glint in her eye. "Though if Joshua Tree doesn't work out, there's always that charming toxic waste dump in Vernon."

Nicole snorted coffee through her nose. "Stop," she gasped, wiping her face with a napkin. "I'll take my chances with the mountain lions."

The café had filled up completely now, the morning rush in full swing. Rosa moved between tables, balancing plates and refilling coffee cups without missing a beat. Through the windows, the fog was starting to burn off, revealing blue sky.

Nicole watched a young couple walk past outside, backpacks slung over their shoulders, probably headed to the beach. There was something freeing about being just another anonymous person in this busy little café, sharing a meal with someone she loved in a place where no one knew their names. Just good food, strong coffee, and the promise of adventure ahead - an adventure she was finally ready to embrace.

She pulled out her phone—not to post, but to book flights home.

Epilogue

Two Years Later

The Temecula Valley Wine & Food Festival buzzed with life under the California sun. The "Dani's Kitchen" food truck, its exterior a bright mosaic of oranges and blues, commanded prime real estate near the festival entrance. The line of waiting customers stretched past three wine stalls, everyone drawn by the smell of grilled meat and fresh tortillas.

Inside the truck, Ana moved with newfound confidence as she assembled each plate, a quiet satisfaction filling her. The dance of service had become second nature—she knew exactly when to start the next batch of tortillas, could predict the exact moment Dani would need fresh cilantro chopped. The cramped space that had once felt overwhelming now felt like home.

"Order up!" she called, sliding two plates of street corn topped with *cotija* and chili lime across the counter. She'd mastered Dani's plating technique—the precise angle of the corn, the artistic drizzle of *crema*, the dusting of *tajin* that made every dish Instagram-worthy, as if they ever had the time to photograph it.

Beside her, Dani commanded the grill with the same authority she'd once wielded in corporate kitchens, but there was something different about her now. A lightness. Freedom. A smile played on Ana's lips as she watched her. This truck was theirs—every recipe, every sauce, every decision made together. They'd built this from nothing, saving tips and working double shifts until they could afford the down payment.

"Baby, can you grab more limes from the cooler?" Dani asked, not looking up from the *carne asada* she was grilling. "We're almost out up here." It was a simple request, but it spoke volumes about how well they understood each other now.

Ana ducked into their storage area, breathing in the familiar mix of citrus and cilantro. A sense of contentment washed over her. They'd learned each other's rhythms here, discovered new sides to their relationship. Ana now knew exactly how to read Dani's mood by the way she wielded her tongs, could tell when she needed space or support just by the set of her shoulders.

As the afternoon rush began to subside, Dani stretched, rolling her shoulders. "God, my feet are killing me," she said. "Want to check out some of the other vendors? Maybe grab something fancy?" She glanced at their dwindling supplies. "We're down to our last few pounds of meat anyway, and I see the wine vendors starting to pack up. Might as well call it a day." A welcome suggestion - Ana's feet were aching too.

Ana did a quick inventory. "Yeah, we're almost out of everything. Good day though—we sold more in six hours than we usually do in two full days at the farmer's market."

A thrill of pride ran through her. They were really making this work.

Dani started wiping down the grill. "Let's close up. I saw some nice olive oils I want to check out before everyone leaves."

They secured the truck, stacking empty containers and storing leftover ingredients. Through the service window, Ana watched other vendors beginning to break down their stalls, the festival's energy shifting from bustling marketplace to end-of-day cleanup. At the craft beer tent, the owner cracked open bottles and passed them around to neighboring vendors. The wine sellers toasted each other with their leftover samples, while the couple who ran the empanada stand collapsed into their folding chairs with cold beers. A sense of camaraderie filled the air, and Ana felt a surge of belonging. They were part of something here, something real and fulfilling.

They made their way through the remaining crowd. Vendors called out discounted prices on their wares—local honey, craft beer, small-batch wines. "How about a plant?" Ana suggested as they passed a display bursting with greenery. "Our kitchen window could use something other than the basil we always kill."

The stall was an oasis of life. One side showcased culinary herbs—everything from classic basil and thyme to rare varieties of mint and sage, their copper tags displaying both cooking suggestions and care instructions. The other side featured a collection of desert plants—succulents in jewel tones, tiny cacti, and drought-resistant flowers. Small terrariums dotted the display, each one a miniature landscape.

Ana's steps slowed as she recognized the two women behind the counter—one blonde, one dark-haired, both sun-kissed and wearing practical clothes. Her jaw dropped slightly. "Nicole? Jen?"

The names left her mouth before she could stop them. The couple looked up, exchanging quick glances before their eyes settled on Ana and Dani. Nicole's hair was shorter now, pulled back in a messy ponytail, her face bare of makeup but glowing with health. Jen stood close beside her, arranging a display of edible flowers.

"I'm Ana," she said, suddenly feeling a bit awkward. "We met at King Ranch a couple years ago. I was working service that weekend."

"The lemonade," Nicole said slowly, recognition dawning. She looked different now, softer somehow. "You brought us lemonade in the garden." She turned to Jen, something passing between them—a shared memory of that difficult day.

"You look different," Ana said, meaning it as a compliment. Gone was the pose, the awareness. In its place was something solid. A glowing tan and a genuine smile.

"I am different. We both are," Nicole said, her hand finding Jen's. "Sometimes I can't believe that was our life. All that pressure, that constant performance..." She shook her head. "This is so much better." She gestured to their diverse display. "Jen grows everything, and I handle the marketing. I don't show my face though. Just honest photos of honest plants." A smile played on Ana's lips - she understood exactly what Nicole meant.

"You're local?" Jen asked, gesturing to Ana's "Dani's Kitchen" t-shirt while she misted a collection of air plants.

"Moved here last year," Ana explained. "One of Dani's dishes went viral—actually viral, not manufactured viral—and suddenly we had wedding venues calling. The food truck came after. Something that's just ours."

"Good for you," Nicole said. "We started with just a few pots in our backyard. Now we supply half the restaurants in the valley with herbs, and our succulents are super popular."

"The chefs love having fresh herbs growing in their kitchens," Jen added. "And the succulent gardens just took off—turns out wine country tourists love a bit of desert beauty."

Dani's attention caught on a small purple-tinged succulent nestled among the herbs. She picked it up, examining its delicate geometry. "This one's beautiful."

"*Echeveria lilacina*," Jen said. "Desert rose. It's one of our hardiest varieties."

"Like us," Dani said to Ana with a cheesy grin. "Growing stronger in difficult conditions." She turned to Jen. "We'll take this one."

"Aww, babe, you're the sweetest." Anna shot her an adoring look and pointed at the Persian mint. "Let's get one of those too, we use a lot of mint."

Jen wrapped both plants carefully, tucking care instructions into each package. "The succulent's on us," she said. "Think of it as a thank you. For being kind that day when everything was falling apart."

* * *

Back home, Dani placed two cold bottles of Corona on the small table. Ana carefully positioned the gifted succulent on the windowsill, next to their new, high-end coffee machine—a splurge they'd allowed themselves after a particularly profitable month.

"You know why I picked this one?" Dani asked, wrapping her arms around Ana's waist from behind.

"Because it's pretty?"

"Because it reminds me of us." Dani rested her chin on Ana's shoulder. "Look how it grows—taking whatever life throws at it and turning it into something beautiful. All those double shifts, all those nights apart, all those struggles to get the truck started… and here we are, still growing, still reaching for the light."

Ana turned in Dani's arms, touched by the unexpected poetry from her usually practical girlfriend. "Who knew my chef was such a romantic?"

"Only with you, baby." Dani pulled her closer. "I love you."

"I love you too." Ana reached for her phone, thinking to capture the moment—the succulent, the two of them together. But instead, she set it aside. Some moments weren't meant to be shared. Some moments were just for them.

Afterword

We hope you've loved reading Reel vs Real as much as we've loved writing it. If you've enjoyed this book, would you consider rating it and reviewing it? Reviews are very important to authors and we'd be really grateful! #BigLove

If you want to be kept up to date on new releases through our monthly newsletters, here's where you can sign up and receive a free novella!

Lise Gold: Newsletter

Ruby Scott: Newsletter

About the Author

Lise Gold is an author of lesbian romance. Her romantic attitude, enthusiasm for travel and love for feel good stories form the heartland of her writing. Born in London to a Norwegian mother and English father, and growing up between the UK, Norway, Zambia and the Netherlands, she feels at home pretty much everywhere and has an unending curiosity for new destinations. She goes by 'write what you know' and is often found in exotic locations doing research or getting inspired for her next novel.

Working as a designer for fifteen years and singing semi-professionally, Lise has always been a creative at heart. Her novels are the result of a quest for a new passion after resigning from her design job in 2018.

When not writing from her kitchen table, Lise can be found cooking, at the gym or singing her heart out somewhere, preferably country or blues. She lives in London with her dogs El Comandante and Bubba.

www.lisegold.com

Also by Lise Gold

Lily's Fire

Beyond the Skyline

The Cruise

French Summer

Fireflies

Northern Lights

Southern Roots

Eastern Nights

Western Shores

Northern Vows

Living

The Scent of Rome

Blue

The Next Life

In The Mirror

Christmas In Heaven

Welcome to Paradise

After Sunset

Paradise Pride

Cupid Is A Cat

Members Only

Along The Mystic River

In Dreams

Chance Encounters

Songbirds of Sedona

Red Rock Ranch

Mistletoe Motel

The Turning Tides of Us

About the Author

Ruby Scott lives in a quiet village nestled in the Scottish hills with her wife, Angie. As an avid reader she got up one day, had an extra cup of coffee, and thought, I'm going to write a book.

It's amazing where an extra cup of coffee can take you, because Ruby has now published over twenty books across her two sapphic pen names, Ruby Scott, and Frankie Duncan.

Endless curiosity combined with a love of traveling and books, Ruby is never without adventure, and she invites you to join her.

www.rubyscott.com

Also by Ruby Scott

Love Trauma

Open Heart

Diagnosis Love

Trails of the Heart

Healing of the Heart

Hot Response

Seconds Out

Inside Fighter

On The Ropes

May I Call You Mistress

Darkness of Desire

Mistress of Desire

Commitment to Desire

The Stranger Within

Strangely Familiar

Rescuing Hearts

Evergreen

No Way Out

www.ingramcontent.com/pod-product-compliance
Ingram Content Group UK Ltd.
Pitfield, Milton Keynes, MK11 3LW, UK
UKHW041011120225
455007UK00001B/8